FOR LOVE OF
Ivy

OTHER PUBLICATIONS BY
SUSAN EVANS McCLOUD

Where the Heart Leads

My Enemy, My Love

Amelia's Daughter

By All We Hold Dear

I'm Going to Be Baptized

Not In Vain

The Heart and the Will

Songs of Life

Black Stars Over Mexico

My Child to Be

First Love, Last Love

Anna

Lady of Mystery

A Vow to Keep

A Dream to Follow

Jennie

Beloved Stranger

Abide the Dark Dawn

Ravenwood

Joseph Smith: A Photo Biography,
The Young Latter-day Saint's Library, Volume 1

FOR LOVE OF
Ivy

A Novel by
Susan Evans McCloud

BOOKCRAFT
Salt Lake City, Utah

All characters in this book
are fictitious, and any resemblance
to actual persons, living or dead,
is purely coincidental.

ISBN 0-88494-873-0

First Paperback Printing, 1993

Printed in the United States of America

To my grandmother, IVY DAVIS EVANS
And to my own mother, DOROTHY...
Whom she loved...

*Each generation gathers together
the imperishable children of the past,
and increases them by new sons of
light, alike radiant with immortality.*

BANCROFT

1

Look where thy love comes;
yonder is thy dear.

SHAKESPEARE

Would he come? Would he be waiting to meet me? This was our final, long descent into the valley. We had crossed Last Creek nineteen times—until our heads grew dizzy, and from the mouth of the canyon gazed down upon the City of the Great Salt Lake.

Earlier I had bathed in the creek water, washed my matted hair, and put on my other dress. It was worn and faded, but at least it would be clean.

There were butterflies in my stomach. Was it just five miles till we reached the valley floor? They seemed to stretch into fifty, and with each step the strange, tight feeling in my throat, the churning inside me, grew stronger.

Jane Graham came up and walked beside me. Her fair English skin was burned a deep copper by the sun, and there were lines and wrinkles around her kindly eyes.

"Your mother should be here," she said simply.

Jane and my mother had been the best of friends for twenty years. They had raised their babies together back in England. I shaded my eyes and swallowed the lump that

1

suddenly came to my throat. Three weeks—if only she could have made it three more weeks!

"I feel she is here," I answered. "Don't you?"

Jane wiped a tear away with her roughened hand.

"Yes, dearie, Meg Simpson wouldn't miss this day for nothin'. She's somewhere here abouts all right, and probably a far sight more comfortable than the two of us, eh, Ivy?"

We walked in silence a moment, then she turned her bright, searching eyes upon me.

"How long is it, Ivy—seven, eight months since you've seen him?"

"Ten months. Ten months, one week, and four days—"

Jane laughed and threw her strong, freckled arms around me. "He'll be there, dearie, don't you fear. He'll be there."

I didn't feel as certain. Ten months was a long time. Sometimes I couldn't even quite remember what he looked like. His voice, that held music and laughter no matter what he was saying; I couldn't quite recall it anymore.

"He's very clever," I found myself replying, "and very handsome. He'll try anything once, and he has that provoking sparkle in his eyes. There must be a lot of pretty girls between here and England."

"Have you no faith in the boy? Shame on you, Ivy!"

It wasn't that. But how could I explain? For ten, long months I had waited for this moment. Nights on the ship and under the wagon, I'd pictured our meeting dozens of ways in my mind. I looked down at my dress, faded and covered already with layers of fine dust. Was my own face as weathered and wrinkled as Jane's?

"I'll braid your hair and wind it the way he likes, hon'." Jane pinched my cheek and her bright eyes began to sparkle. "I've still got a trick or two up my sleeve. I'll have you all prettied up for Hamlet. Don't you worry!"

A new wagon train entering the valley was cause for excitement. Our arrival must have been heralded for there were hundreds of people gathered to greet us. Groups of fresh-faced children skipped from wagon to wagon, curious to stare their fill at the newcomers. For a moment or two, I forgot about watching for Hamlet. Everywhere I looked there was so much to see! The valley sprawled, long and wide, pulling the eye with it toward the wall of circling mountains on the west and the thin, silver line which I took to be the salt water lake. There were no green meadows with wide-spreading trees, but large stretches of fields had been planted, houses built, and lots laid out with gardens and young trees. There was a feeling of freedom and promise in the air.

Suddenly, all about me people were finding one another. I stood and watched mother embrace daughter, friend embrace friend, and an aching for my own mother caught inside me. Tears, much to my frustration, blurred my eyes. I wanted to belong here, but I felt myself a stranger—apart and alone.

I didn't recognize the young man pushing his way toward me. He wore rough clothing and a short, trim beard with a thin mustache. His hair, bleached by the desert sun, was light and mottled. Nothing about him was familiar—until he looked at me and held me with his eyes. Then my breath caught painfully in my throat.

He was lean and hardened, and taller than I remembered, moving with a lithe sureness, swallowing up the distance between us. He threw back his fair head and laughed, and the sound washed over me with a sweet, tingling sensation. He paused as he reached me and stood, leaning easily back on his heels, to observe me with warm, appraising eyes. I met his gaze with a growing sense of warmth and elation, and I saw the casual manner leave him and a look come into his eyes; a new look I had never seen there before. I couldn't describe it, but I can still feel the sense of warmth and love and tenderness it gave me.

He moved closer and touched my hair with a tentative hand. Then his lips found mine with the same sweetness and tenderness I had seen in his eyes. When he drew back, reluctantly, his eyes were sparkling again. He stroked his red-blonde beard self-consciously.

"I'll shave it off if it bothers you, Ivy."

His voice! How could I have forgotten one note of that musical voice?

"I like the beard," I said, reaching out to touch it.

"Ivy, how can you be prettier than I remember? I was sure when I saw you again I'd take one look and ask myself, 'Whatever in the world attracted you to this girl?'"

He was teasing me. It had always been his greatest delight to tease me!

"Where's your mother," he asked, "off gossiping with Janie Graham? After four thousand miles of sand and ocean, haven't those two had enough of each other?"

As soon as the words were out, he knew the answer. He could see it in my face and my eyes.

Hamlet is a sensitive man. He didn't try to comfort me with awkward words, he just pulled me close against him and let me cry. In the midst of that noise and confusion, those hundreds of busy people, he stood and held me, and he seemed to lend some of his strength and serenity to me.

For the first time some of the pain inside me healed. Home wasn't the rain-washed countrysides of England, or even this awesome, uncivilized desert where we stood. Home was the little circle of his arms. I knew this as I had never known it before. I was home in his arms; there was nothing else that mattered.

2

Sole partner,
and sole part of all my joy,
dearer thyself than all.

MILTON

My wedding day dawned cloudless and clear, the dry, breathless sun of the desert taking its time to skim over the peaks of the mountains then hang, a hard, shimmering disk in the blue of the sky.

Rows of dugouts had been thrown up as temporary shelter for new arrivals, though I shuddered sometimes wondering how long "temporary" would mean to some of the poorer families. It was incredible to me, as I gazed out upon the fresh, still morning, that after living sixteen years in the large, stone farmhouse of my father—cool and clean, with wide fireplaces and leaded windows—I could be standing stooped in a narrow hut, without father or mother, preparing myself ever so simply for my own wedding.

It all seemed so very alien then. My father had never even known this vast desert existed. He had died of the marsh fever before the Mormon Elders ever found our farm, ate mother's warm bread, thick cheese and cool milk, and changed our lives with the message they brought.

My brother Thomas, strong for his age and dependable, had held the farm together after father had died. That farm had been his life. He loved it, and didn't take kindly to the idea of anything changing. So he didn't sit and listen when the Elders talked. Even so, he hadn't been harsh, and when mother made her decision to join the Church, then to come to Zion, he tried to understand it as best he could, and he stood beside her because he knew that was what she needed him to do.

I pulled out my mother's gilt-framed mirror and held it before me. Perhaps she had looked into this very mirror on her own wedding day. Three generations of Wesley women had gazed in that mirror, looking into their own faces and their own eyes: first my grandmother, then my mother, and now myself ... mother become a Simpson, and I to shortly become a wife with a different name. I looked searchingly. There were no freckles to mar my skin and my thick, brown hair, so brown it was nearly black, was brushed and lay smooth and silky against my cheek. In that poor light my eyes looked black, almost sullen. People had told me my whole life that my own deep, large eyes were the image of my mother. And so that morning as I looked deep into those uncertain eyes staring back at me, I tried hard to see my mother's image there as well as mine.

I thought, laying the mirror down gently, *I wish mother could have known all this.* She would have been enchanted with the desert and the sage, the clear cold mountain streams, the space, the challenge. I felt the hot tears gathering behind my eyes. *Mother, how can I be married without you!*

Jane was coming! I could hear her voice, her laughter. She was coming, with her kind, capable hands to help me. I brushed the tears aside and shook back my hair. I knew what she would say if she caught me crying.

"Come, come now, love. Don't you know 'tis bad luck for a girl to cry on her wedding day? We'll have none of this. Your mother wouldn't want it."

6

I picked up the mirror and held it at arm's length. The solemn face with the deep brown eyes that met my gaze said nothing, but the eyes were my mother's—and the nose, and the fine, high forehead. When at last the eyes warmed and smiled, it was her eyes smiling, and I turned with that smile to greet what the day would bring.

Hamlet came for me himself in his father's light wagon. His hair and beard were trimmed and the suit he was wearing gave him a look of gentility. He hardly resembled the frontiersman who had met our arrival into the valley two weeks before. He took my hand and helped me into the wagon, touching my fingers a little lingeringly. His eyes were dancing, but his face was unusually solemn. I watched his profile beside me as we rode.

Could it really be true that tonight he would be my husband? I would go home with him, and never leave him again. We would sleep together and eat together; get up in the morning together, work together. I would learn more of him, much more than I knew right now. And he would know all the secrets of my heart; all the womanly things that I barely knew myself. I felt a thrill run through me, warm at first, then chilling. This was what I had wanted for so long. I wasn't really frightened, but fulfillment loomed too near, closing now within my grasp—yet still so unknown!

I had wished for a temple, a proper place to be married. But as I stood with Hamlet and heard the sacred words, as I watched the light leap into his eyes when he looked at me, as I realized we would be sealed now forever, I needed nothing more than that moment, with his hand touching mine.

There was a surprise celebration after the wedding. Jane and Emma, Hamlet's mother, had conspired together. We had a splendid cake and cold, apple cider and a fancy kind of bread I had never tasted. In truth, I was too excited to really taste a thing, but my heart was warmed by their kindness and attention.

Hamlet's father pulled me tight, rocking me back and forth as he hugged me. Daniel Drummond had hugged me that way ever since I had been a little girl. But this time I sensed a difference, something between us. I was no longer the innocent child he had played with for I belonged to Hamlet, and thus to him. I was wife to his oldest son, and that made the difference. His eyes held much the same tenderness Hamlet's did, and when I stood on tiptoe to kiss him, they misted over with fine tears.

Emma was not a demonstrative person. She was the reticent Englishwoman to the bone. But she hugged me gently and said against my hair,

"I've never wanted him to marry anyone but you, Ivy."

So I moved in the warming glow of my happiness, trying to prolong the lovely hour, postponing the time of going "home" with Hamlet. We were to share his parents' cabin until ours was built, and so our home would not be ours alone. It was that which I somehow could not face, not yet.

Finally though, the time came and Hamlet took my hand and lifted me into the wagon. His hands closing on my waist felt lean, strong and warm. This scene had happened already, just hours before. But then I was only a girl, and now I was a wife. And now Hamlet was mine for ever and ever.

He took the wagon slowly through the city, and I was content to bask in the warmth of his presence, enjoying my own feelings and sensations. After awhile I roused to look about me and realized we were driving through scenes new and unknown to me.

"Where are you taking us, Hamlet?" I asked.

He only cocked his head and wouldn't answer.

What surprise did he have in store? I wondered.

Soon we left the city and, picking up speed, passed even the outlying homesteads as we approached the rounding hills. My curiosity grew as Hamlet turned the horses up a narrow path and the close-growing brush of the mountains closed about us. It was dark there, evening was fast approaching, and the cool silence only increased my anticipation.

Suddenly a clearing opened before us with a tiny cabin hugging the cliff. I caught my breath. The view was splendid, and a cold and winding mountain stream gurgled at our feet. I touched Hamlet's arm, not knowing how to express my wonder and pleasure. He lifted me from the wagon, high into the air, then cradled me in his arms like a child while I wound my arms around his neck and laughed.

He carried me across the threshold of the cabin, then carefully set me on my feet and kissed me.

"No bride should have to spend her wedding night with her husband's parents," he said softly.

"Hamlet!" I cried, "this is perfect. Whose cabin is this? How did you ever arrange it?"

His eyes were spilling over with delight.

"I have my ways," he answered, then bent and piled wood in the small, rock fireplace and deftly built a fire to light the gloom. I watched his sure, graceful movements and felt thoroughly warm and happy and secure.

That evening, Hamlet caught fresh fat trout in the nearby stream, we roasted them over the fire, and ate them with the bread and cider Jane had tucked in among our things. It seemed we had the rest of forever to ourselves! We sat by the fire far into the night and fashioned a dozen dreams for our tomorrows and drew out the sweet, clear memories of yesterday like the trinkets from a treasure box of pleasures.

"I remember the first time I saw you," Hamlet teased. "You were nothing more than a gangly little girl, staring at me with enormous, brown eyes."

"That's not true! It was you who stared at me."

"I suppose you're right," he admitted. "I thought you

the prettiest girl I had ever seen and didn't really guess how young you were."

"I was twelve," I defended.

"Twelve!" he repeated, his voice filled with merry scorn. "I was a man of sixteen, and young men don't go about courting little girls. I was a laughingstock to everyone I knew."

"I tried desperately to grow up," I said, remembering. "I was so afraid you wouldn't wait, that you'd marry someone else."

"You shouldn't have worried," he said, growing serious. "I've never loved any woman but you, Ivy."

Woman—he called me a woman! It gave me an aching sensation deep inside. I was not yet seventeen, and I still felt so much like a young, awkward girl. Even when his eyes grew dark and he drew me to him, I was painfully aware of my youth and ignorance. But he held me gently as the fire burned low and faded. He was patient and tender, so that I forgot my fears and remembered only how dearly I loved him, unmindful of everything else in the pleasure of loving him.

Three flawless days and nights we spent in that cabin. Our last evening we sat beside the fire as before.

"I've found the perfect spot to build a home," Hamlet announced.

"Where?" I asked eagerly.

"It's not in the city," he replied.

"Well, where then?"

"It's not even in the valley," he said more quietly, looking up with a rare uneasiness in his eyes. "You like it here, don't you? Here, in this cabin?"

"Hamlet, you're talking in riddles."

"Listen, Ivy. The Salt Lake Valley's getting crowded. More and more people pour into it every day. It's destined to be a city; a big, sprawling city."

"So?" I asked. "That seems wonderful to me."

I did love Brigham's city. There were not only plots and houses, farms and gardens, but mills and stores and shops. States goods sold cheaper than they did back east. There was even talk of building a sugar plant. It was much more than I had hoped to find here, knowing it was only four short years since the first pioneers had arrived.

"There's another valley south of here, over the mountains," continued Hamlet.

"You've been there?" I asked, and watched the light leap into his eyes.

"Several times. There are new settlements, Ivy, up and down the valley. President Young has asked for families to go there."

He paused.

I smiled a little and he went on.

"It's a lush, green valley, Ivy. There's a fresh-water lake and acres of fertile farmland. And room—"

I couldn't help laughing.

"Room!" I said. "Hamlet, I don't understand. You lived in England until you were grown, on a postage stamp of land that didn't even belong to you. Now, suddenly, this whole, wide valley isn't enough!"

"This land gets into your skin, Ivy. I've got this need to push out on my own—where no one else has paved the way before me, or laid down rules they expect me to follow."

I had grown up with Hamlet, you might say. I knew him well, or at least I thought I did, but this big, untamed land had a way of changing a man—bringing out something strong and untamed in himself, which might have otherwise lain fallow and untouched.

He reached for my hand, and I could feel his longing.

"It's a place like this—a little, sheltered valley, snug up against the bottom of the mountains. There's a creek, Ivy, and trees—cottonwoods, scrub oak, and a few slender willows. Sunflowers cover the ground like a golden blanket."

It did sound beautiful as he described it.

"But what will we do when we need something, Hamlet? What about doctors and flour mills—and schools?"

I was groping, and he could sense it.

"I'll take care of you, Ivy! Those things will come-eventually. But you and I will be first! We'll start it and build it and watch it grow, and someday when our sons and daughters ask us, we'll tell them that you and I were the first white people to set foot there. No one else plowed or planted or built before us. That's some kind of gift to give your children, Ivy."

Children! A cold little doubt clutched at my heart. I must be able to have the children he wanted!

Hamlet was so earnest, so intense that my heart melted. How could I say no to the man I loved when he looked at me with those little-boy eyes?

"Three days ago I placed my life into your keeping," I said as I met his searching gaze. "I trusted you then, Hamlet. I still trust you now."

He held me against him, crushing me without knowing.

"You won't be sorry, Ivy. You won't be sorry!"

I forced away my doubts and my own desires for I could read the happy promise in his eyes, and, foolish as it might have been, I believed him!

3

*Love wrought
these miracles!*

SHAKESPEARE

When the time came for leaving, it was easier than I'd hoped. Hamlet was like a boy going off on holiday, so strong and sure of himself that his confidence spread. His four, small brothers stood watching enviously. They were all too young to go with him, but they looked at what he was doing as a great adventure, and they longed to share in it somehow.

Hamlet's mother had lost two sons between England and the valley, and I wondered if she felt as though she were losing another one now. Whatever doubts or fears Daniel Drummond might have been feeling, he wisely kept them to himself. His son needed his support now, not his censure. He shook Hamlet's hand, then turned and kissed me.

"It's a stingy thing you're doing, boy. That's all I'll say. Bring this pretty, young thing into the family, then snatch her away before we can fair enjoy her."

Everyone smiled and that eased things a little. I squeezed his hand as it rested against my arm.

Saying goodbye to Jane was, of course, the hardest. It was like saying goodbye to my mother all over again. I

13

realized with a sudden feeling of panic that I had never been without one or the other of them hovering over me, filling my every need, comforting my disappointments, and cheering my gloom. Hamlet was Hamlet, but he couldn't fill that place. I realized then that in some ways I would be all alone.

Before leaving the city, Hamlet stopped at one of the dry goods stores. He said there were some last-minute supplies he needed to replenish, but I smiled, remembering that this was the place where he had discovered what he called "the finest rifle man has ever made." He had held it almost caressingly in his hands, examining each precision-made part, each line, each moulding with an almost awesome appreciation. I knew how badly he wanted to own that rifle. I watched him through the store's glass window now as he picked it up, sighted down the barrel, and then seemed to smooth the fine wood with his hand. I knew that in this country a man's gun was like a good, right arm, and Hamlet deserved to have a gun he could depend on.

He moved out of my view and I closed my eyes, enjoying the warmth, the sense of peace surrounding me, and listened to the quiet sounds he made as he packed his purchases into the back of the wagon.

When he climbed back into the wagon I touched his hand and smiled.

"I'm glad you got the rifle, Hamlet. I think we need it."

He looked at me a moment, then kissed my cheek before he turned to start up the horses.

It wasn't long before the city fell behind us and man's encroachment on the land ended abruptly. The grey-green sagebrush thrived without disturbance. The great, granite peaks rose immovable, unconcerned. The height, the space, the immensity seemed overpowering, and the beauty so raw, so splendid, that I caught my breath and found myself turning and twisting and craning my neck to catch one last glimpse of this scene or that.

As we climbed out of the valley, we looked back at a

lovely view of the city, which seemed from this distance to be a mere impress in the broad land with the blue Salt Lake and Antelope Island beyond. The Jordan Valley stretched away to one side, sunny and open, framed by a line of mountains at its edge.

When we dropped down into the Utah Valley, Hamlet's excitement mounted and so did mine. There were several little settlements already started: Grove Creek, Dry Creek, and, further yet, Hobble Creek. Along these streams were clumps of green brush and trees that made it easy for the eye to follow their course across the land. The last settlement to the south was the fort at Pacen. It was nearest our destination, so we had planned to stop there and stay for a season while Hamlet built a cabin at the spot he had chosen for us.

We were seven days on the road together, and they were good days: the weather was fair, the roadways dry, and Hamlet and I were filled with the adventure of our new life together. Nevertheless, I was relieved as we neared the little fort, for I was anxious for a warm bath, a bed indoors, and the company of other women. August is the hottest month on the desert, and my lungs felt like they had been coated with quarts of sand. I had sand in my hair and in my eyes and under the nails of my hands.

Pacen, in that summer of 1851, housed 300 to 400 people. The settlement was enclosed in a fort on both sides of Peteetneet Creek and surrounded by a tall, picket fence, higher than a man could reach. Many farms, cleared of sagebrush, boasted healthy fields and gardens. There was even a schoolhouse, newly built, with rows of little, glass windows! I was delighted, and couldn't help thinking of children of my own someday learning their lessons at that pretty school.

I wanted children desperately, and pushed aside the fear that I might have trouble. My own mother had borne only my brother and myself, though she had tried and lost half a dozen other babies. That couldn't happen with me. Hamlet and I wanted lots and lots of children!

Hamlet pulled the wagon to a halt and leapt down. He seemed to have as much eagerness and energy as he had had when our journey had begun, and I wished I could have been like him. I felt tired and drained, anxious to exchange the jolting rhythm of the wagon for solid ground. I clambered down and stood by the wagon as I waited for Hamlet to return with someone from the fort.

I felt at home in Pacen from the start. Hamlet and I stayed with Widow Porter and her old, blind father, Phineas. In exchange, Hamlet helped with the stock and with repairs on the cabin, chopped the wood, and handled the early harvest. I too helped around the place and learned much about pioneer housewifery under Lydia Porter's capable tutelage.

Poor Phineas was good for little more than meddling. Indeed, rambling and absent-minded as he was, and totally unadjusted to his blindness, he could be counted on to get into some kind of trouble every time you turned your back. Once, mistaking a bowl of thick starch to contain drippings and scraps for the hogs, he padded out and fed it to them. He also insisted on gathering eggs from the chickens, although he broke almost as many as he managed to salvage. Once, while carrying a bucket full of three dozen eggs, he bumped right into the well and the eggs ended as an inglorious puddle around his feet.

He trailed disaster with him as his daily fare, though a quaint and very comical kind of disaster, to be sure. Once, trying to help his daughter plant the garden, he sowed six rows of beans where the onions were planted, and radishes over the peas before she stopped him. Impossible, but delightful, he redeemed himself by being a veritable master at storytelling. Many an evening I sat unashamedly at his knee with the hoard of little children gathered there, and while his voice lasted and his thoughts spun out, forgot the fabric of my own existence, and was content to be immersed in whatever world his magic created.

As the days passed, I knew I would have been more than content to settle within the fort, but Hamlet's heart was set.

The place Hamlet had chosen for our home was just four miles south of Pacen, but it seemed to me that four miles out alone in that wild land might as well have been four hundred.

But I had promised, and the land *was* beautiful to behold.

Fertile fields hugged a low, green hillside, a winding creek widened into a pond, and there were birds and trees and cooling canyon breezes. When first I stood upon the spot with Hamlet, I felt a sense of peace, a certain rightness about our being there. I could see more than the cabin Hamlet was building. I could see a large, substantial house with windows and two chimneys and a porch, a big red barn, a smokehouse and a hen coop, and an orchard with a tree swing for the children. I think that Hamlet saw the vision too—his lush green fields, his farm, his future. But first there were the fields to clear of sagebrush, and the little cabin walls to be raised and roofed.

When he wasn't helping at the fort, Hamlet spent his days out at the homestead. The men were good at helping one another though, and so the days that Hamlet worked about the fort were made up by the help the men gave him on our place.

The first time the men went hunting small game together, I noticed that Hamlet wasn't carrying his new rifle. When I rememberd to ask him about it, he smiled and cocked his head.

"I never said I bought that rifle, Ivy. 'Twas you said that."

"But I saw you," I objected.

"You saw me what?" he asked with that sparkle in his eyes.

He was right. I had only seen him looking at the rifle. I never saw him pack it into the wagon. Nor had I been there when he had later unloaded the wagon.

"Well, if you didn't buy the rifle, what did you buy?"

He wasn't about to answer that question yet, and I'd learned by then that it was no use to hurry Hamlet.

Sometimes Hamlet stayed out at the cabin site for several days together. I missed him at those times with a fierce loneliness, in spite of the busy days and the stories that Phineas told. Nights were the hardest—crawling beneath the quilts, missing the warmth of him lying there beside me, and missing his laughing voice as he recounted the day's adventures and shared with me the hours we'd spent apart. Lydia said she'd never seen two such love birds, and the fact that we were newly married didn't even excuse it.

"You've stumbled across one piece of good luck," she told me. "You've found a man who adores the ground you walk on, loves you to the point of silliness. Way I figure, that's better'n station or money."

"Why?" I asked with curiosity.

"Every woman needs that kind of love, hon'. There just aren't many lucky enough to find it."

August slipped away into September, still bright and hot with the breathless, desert dryness. And, breathlessly, I found what I had anticipated was really true: I was with child! Already it had happened—so easily, in spite of all my worries! Lydia, I think, must have suspected, for I was far more surprised at the fact than she was.

"It's a good, healthy way to start a marriage," she insisted.

Even so, I was frightened. I was so ignorant in the ways of women. And how was I to tell the news to Hamlet?

I tried several times, but he worked long, hard hours

and seemed always tired, and even a little preoccupied—or so I reasoned. Though I knew all I needed was to ask for his attention and I would have it instantly.

Then one night we were walking alone together, by the edge of the creek, looking off toward our land.

"It's just a matter of days till the cabin's done now." Hamlet's voice held a note of tired satisfaction.

"I think sometimes you push yourself too hard."

He ran a hand through his light, silken hair and grinned at me.

"I want you to myself, Ivy. Lydia has been marvelous, and I can't even complain about the old man—but we need to be alone again." He pulled me gently against him. "Don't you agree?"

I felt my heart beat more rapidly.

"Yes ... yes, we'd better make good use of the time while we have it."

He held me back and stared at me quizically.

"While we have it? What's this? Are you planning on running away?"

"No," I said, feeling foolish.

"Well, neither am I."

He thoughtfully rubbed his narrow beard and regarded me with rougish eyes.

"Though there is this little Ute squaw down by the river. She has big, brown eyes and long, raven-black hair—and the way she looks at me—well, sometimes I get to thinking—"

I flew at him.

"You're awful, Hamlet, you're shameful! Teasing me this way—"

He caught my flailing arms and held them against him. The grin was still there, but his eyes had grown serious.

"I couldn't resist it, Ivy. After all, once you become a mother and all grown up, you might not let me tease you anymore."

He paused a moment, then continued more gently. "That is what you're trying to tell me, isn't it?"

I nodded and looked deep into his eyes.

"Are you frightened, too?" I asked him.

"Of course I am! Things like this are bound to scare a man."

"I worry about the baby already," I said.

"The baby! It's not the baby I'm worried about."

"Me?" I cried, feeling foolishly happy inside. "Oh, Hamlet, I'll be all right. Women have babies every day, why—"

"So they do, but you're just a slip of a girl. It's hard work homesteading." He knit his brow. "You'll have to be careful, Ivy."

"Are you sorry? Do you wish there wasn't a baby yet, do you—"

"No! No, no." He took my face in his hands and kissed me. "I'm sorry, Ivy. I never meant that. I want the child. It will make you more a part of me than ever. It's a miracle, weaving our lives together, and out of that oneness creating another life."

I held my breath. He had never spoken like this before—never let me see quite so deep inside.

"I love you, Hamlet," I said, drawing him to me.

He nodded, and though I couldn't read the look in his eyes, I knew he understood that those words held for me everything I was feeling.

"That was the first miracle," he answered softly. "This baby's the second miracle you've brought me."

4

*I cannot speak enough of this
content; It stops me here;
it is too much of joy ...*

SHAKESPEARE

It was ten o'clock in the morning and I still wasn't feeling any better. Usually the awful queasiness had passed by then, but I gritted my teeth and turned to knead the bread dough even though the sour smell of the yeast made my stomach turn. It was then that I heard it—the unmistakable thudding of beating drums, and the high, yet almost gutteral wailing of Indian women. I turned toward the sound and my muscles tightened. I had harbored a secret fear of the Indians, and dreaded those times when they wandered into the fort.

The warriors, in gaudy paint and wearing bright feathers, gathered in circles and danced their tribal dances. By some compelling fascination, I was drawn toward them while the fear that ran like shivers along my back kept me always at a wide, safe distance back.

I marveled at the apparent ease of the other women about the fort when the squaws made their rounds, asking in quiet voices, "Bread? Any bread?" The women would welcome them into their cabins, talk and ask questions, offer them chairs to sit on, and even let them hold and cuddle the children. But I grew panicky when one of them came too close, and I had to fight against the urge to turn and run.

That particular morning I wiped my hands and walked to the door to see how close to our cabin they were coming. Lydia was out in the garden and Phineas was right in the midst of the dancing warriors so that several had to dodge him as they danced about. I was amazed at how easily, how gracefully they maneuvered, and how almost matter-of-factly they accepted the blind, old white man and his ways.

I must have stood watching longer than I intended, for I was suddenly aware of someone beside me, and turned to see an Indian standing there. Not one of the squat, quiet squaws, but a tall, young warrior. He stood staring at me with paint-rimmed, piercing black eyes. I caught my breath and retreated within the doorway, but he moved too, in one, quick, graceful motion, and rested beside me, grinning merrily.

The feeling of panic clutched at my stomach. I had never been so close to an Indian brave before, and I couldn't help observing his appearance. He wore a fine, new-looking set of fringed, leather leggings and he seemed to stretch his legs and almost prance there beside me, rather than standing still. He thrust out his painted chest and pointed to himself, then wagged his finger at me as the big grin on his face widened. He had fine, white teeth and a handsome sort of face, and his hair was held back with a studded strip of leather, but it was thick and long and bobbed about his shoulders as he moved and gestured. He began talking and calling noisily, and I was afraid to go in for fear that he would follow.

Much to my relief, a crowd began to gather. I was sure someone would relieve me of him, but no one moved. They just stood there happily watching! My handsome, young friend, I soon realized, loved the attention. He preened and strutted and performed before the people, keeping up a

22

constant chatter all the while.

Suddenly, I was struck with an idea. It would only take a moment. I slid through the door, found what I wanted, and returned just as my dusky cavalier had noticed my absence and was whirling about to find me.

I stepped out beside him and held up an oval-shaped looking glass, a smaller mirror than my mother's old one, a gift in fact, from Hamlet before we ever left England. I moved it around to catch the rays of the sun as my friend stood still and stared at the bright patterns of spots the mirror created. I held it up so he could see his face, and I almost wanted to laugh at his wide-eyed, startled expression. I extended the mirror out further and gestured to him, until he understood I intended it for him. With amazement on his face, he reached out and snatched it, then turned it over and over in his hands. He held it close to his nose, then far away, then off to one side, fascinated with his own image.

I felt someone touch me from behind and whirled about to find Hamlet there. He put his arm protectingly round my waist, and I leaned with weak gratitude against him.

My proud, young brave noticed Hamlet too. He pointed to Hamlet, then walked close and pointed to me, and the broad grin broke over his features again.

"Ah, white man's squaw," he muttered, nodding his head briskly up and down.

Hamlet nodded back and the two men laughed together—a hearty, happy sound. The brave stepped closer and pumped Hamlet's hand up and down, then in his haughty manner turned to me, and grasped my hand in his and shook it wildly.

As his firm, warm hand closed over mine I think I shrieked a little; I know that I was trembling all over. With one, fine, graceful jump he bounded off, clutching the precious mirror in his hand.

Lydia was suddenly at my side, but instead of showing

23

horror on her features, she was grinning almost as widely as the brave, and I realized with a shock that she had been laughing.

"He was trying to bargain for you, Ivy. He knew you were a new squaw at the fort—"

"You mean—"

"Yes! He wanted to find out who your father was and buy you for one of his wives!"

The little group that had gathered about us laughed with Lydia—even Hamlet was laughing.

"Only Twinkling Toes would be brash enough for that!"

Suddenly I felt that I would faint. I closed my eyes, hoping the weakness would pass.

"How clever of you to think of the mirror, Ivy!" Lydia beamed at me.

I tried to smile back.

"Yes," someone echoed, "that was just the thing to please him."

Everyone added their congratulations. Hamlet's face was fairly smeared with pride, and it struck me suddenly that no one knew I was afraid—not even Hamlet. They thought I was very clever and very brave; one of the bravest women at the fort. And there was Hamlet, so proud of his clever wife. I wanted to cry on his shoulder, but I realized I couldn't. I couldn't let him know what a coward I was. I couldn't spoil things. I tugged at his arm.

"Please, Hamlet. I've got to sit down."

"Of course," he said after a moment's pause, "the baby!"

He waved to the group and led me inside to a chair.

"Ivy, you were marvelous out there! You'll be the talk of the valley from one end to the other. You and our haughty feathered Indian."

I smiled and let him carry on a little. At last the people outside went away, things calmed down, and Hamlet went back to work.

I told Lydia I was sick, and that was true, but it wasn't so much a sickness as it was fear. In spite of all the praise and attention, in spite of the humor that even I could see, the hard, unreasoning fear wouldn't go away. I hated myself for my weakness, and I cringed at the fact that now there was no one to share it. It was a secret I'd chosen to carry all alone.

At last the cabin was ready for us. The barn was raised, and the animals Hamlet had purchased all safely installed; the chickens were even in the coop. It only lacked us to make it into a home.

Hamlet had been working around the clock. It showed in the tired circles under his eyes, in the way he would fall asleep over his dinner. But he was anxious to move in and get things underway, to harvest the grass hay and the fields of alfalfa he'd planted. So, though overworked and exhausted, he was happy.

It was different for me. I dislike farewells, and this one wasn't easy. I wanted to go with Hamlet—I just didn't want to have to leave to do it! You like to have your cake and eat it too, my mother would have told me, and it was true. I hated to leave those people. I desperately wanted to be alone with Hamlet—but not so really alone that there would be no one else to talk to, no one near. It was wretched.

Lydia seemed calm, and that helped me a little, but poor Phineas didn't seem to understand.

"You hurry back now, child. We'll miss you. Don't stay too long."

Finally I gave up trying to explain, and merely kissed him. There were others too, and I said goodbye to them all. Then Hamlet was there with the wagon and I climbed inside, trying hard not to cry as we waved and pulled away.

It was really a fitting day for this new beginning. It was my birthday—my seventeenth birthday. If I felt a little stab of disappointment, I squelched it with a good talking to myself. I couldn't be angry with Hamlet for forgetting. His days these past few weeks had run into each other; he kept track only in tasks still left to be done, and hours remaining before the darkness stopped him and he stumbled into bed for a brief respite, to be up before the sun could awaken him. He had too many things on his mind. Tonight I would tell him. Alone in the quiet we could celebrate together.

Though I thought he was in a hurry, Hamlet drove slowly. He stopped for some odds and ends at George Hancock's Mercantile, then at another place to check on some stock he wanted to buy. We wound through the valley slowly, companionably, and took a pretty little detour where we stopped and rested, ate big chunks of bread, and drank cold spring water.

When we neared the cabin, I felt my pulse grow faster. As soon as Hamlet stopped the wagon I was out, anxious to examine things myself! As I looked about me I drew in my breath in astonishment.

The cabin actually had a stout, front door, caulked and fitted, and off to the right, with a box of flowers beneath it, fitted snugly into the wall, shone a little window! A real glass window—but how had it come to be there?

Then suddenly I understood. I whirled back toward Hamlet, caught him by surprise, and kissed him wildly. I could see his own deep pleasure in his eyes.

"The gun?" I whispered softly, and he nodded. "But why didn't you buy the gun? It was more important."

"I don't think so," he answered in his simple, straightforward way. "I have guns that will do for our purposes just fine. I don't really need another gun."

He grinned that boyish grin I love so well.

"I figured you'd need the window, Ivy. I don't want you shut up in the cabin, not seeing the sun—or the snow—or the flowers that pop up after the rain."

"I can watch you coming in from the fields at night," I exclaimed, "and wave goodbye every time you have to leave."

"That's right." He swung his lean arm wide around. "All this is yours. You have a right to see it and enjoy it."

I hugged him again, but his mood seemed to change and he placed a bundle of bedding into my hands.

"Run inside with that, Ivy. I'll be right along."

So it happened just as everyone had planned it. I pushed open the new, stiff door and walked inside—straight into the arms of two dozen, anxious people who shouted and sang and tried to hug me all at once.

"Happy birthday, Ivy. Happy birthday!"

"You see, we fooled her!"

"Surprise! Surprise! Oh dear, is she going to cry?"

They were right. It was all I could do to hold back the tears. I'd never had so much love from so many people. I didn't know how to handle it all at once. And Hamlet—how I adored him at that moment!

We had a marvelous party, eating our fill of meat and stew, of puddings and pies and breads. We laughed and sang and admired Hamlet's handiwork, and I think the only mishap of the day came when Phineas poured salt on his apple pie because he thought the tart apples wanted a little sugar.

There were presents, too: quilts and sugar and new soap from some of the women. Lydia had made curtains for the new window from a length of blue chintz she had once caught me admiring. Brother Hancock even gave us two of his prized peach stones to plant. There was such a spirit of sharing and concern.

They left us with food enough for the rest of the week, and a warmth that filled every corner of the new cabin—a kind of benediction on our home. I vowed then that I would hug that spirit of loving and never chase it away by angry words, or by any mean, little ways. Hamlet could work on the desert and make it blossom, but inside those four walls I would keep alive the lovely, singing happiness of that day.

5

Woulds't have we weep?
Why, now thou hast thy will . . .

SHAKESPEARE

Our first few days in the cabin were leisurely spent and sweet. There was the honeymoon feeling we had known in that other cabin, a sense of romance and renewal which both of us needed. We hung the curtains and organized the room until every little thing was the way we wanted.

The cabin was comprised of one, large room, with a lean-to where I cooked that had a wide chimney place where pine logs blazed. There were whitewashed walls and a clean, canvas ceiling where the play of the fire wove patterns of shadow and light. Our sturdy, four-poster bedstead stood in one corner, the fat feather mattress spread with my own patchwork counterpane. A small, rag carpet lay in a special place on the floor, warming my feet whenever I walked across it. Lydia's clean, chintz curtains hung across my window, and Hamlet had built bracket shelves here and there, which I covered with white cloth, edged with knitted lace. Here we placed the few ornaments we had, and our books: the Bible and the Book of Mormon, a volume of poetry, Shakespeare, and *Pilgrim's Progress*. The small, round table where we ate boasted a calico cover, and we had several wooden chairs, as well as my rocker. Two chests, a washstand, and of course, my mother's old, mahogany dresser. To me it seemed a palace, and all of it mine! My heart seemed to skip in delight as I just gazed 'round it.

After the house was settled, we carefully planted Brother Hancock's peach stones, and brought out the rosebush shoots that my mother had so lovingly nurtured during our long journey—shoots cut carefully from her own rosebushes back in England.

Just planting them made me miss my mother dearly, and I wondered with a certain impatience of spirit if she could possibly watch what we were doing here. This new land wasn't home to her; she had never seen it. She wouldn't see the child I was to bear—she would never be a part of my experiences in this life again! I'll admit I rather hovered over the roses; even remembered them in my prayers, if the truth were known. I had so few tangible reminders left of my mother, and I wanted those roses to stay with me through the years, their fragrance and beauty reminding me of her.

When Hamlet went back to work, he went back in earnest, stretching the days even longer than before. But there was no one for me to work with and talk with, and I experienced my first, real taste of loneliness. I tried hard to keep busy, to take comfort in the things around me. Even on the desert, autumn is a lovely time of year. With so few trees, each leaf became a treasure. The prettiest ones I found I brought in and pressed, or arranged them with some squash and gourds in a basket for the table.

Sometimes, alone with the silence and the space, I would become suddenly aware of the hills and high peaks around me. I could almost feel the strength of the lean, grey rocks as they stood there, ancient, immovable. Such times brought a surge of excitement, a feeling of power that welled up inside of me, as though I had part in the power of this wild land. And the wonder of it all would strike me again: this is where I shall live and make my home and bear my children. This is what my children shall grow up knowing—dust and black rock, lavish sunsets that streak the sky, gurgling creeks and red-skinned Indians; not the clipped lawns, the deep, silent rivers of my own childhood. This they would love; and this would fashion their lives. This would be "home" to them. And I? I should live out my life and die in this immense and alien place.

In late October the rains began. At first I thought, *well, at least they'll drive Hamlet inside*. But I soon learned there were dozens of things he could do in spite of the rain. Hamlet! He didn't mind the wet and the gloom. I'd never run across a man, a beast or anything in the elements that could discourage or even dampen him. How I longed for his high spirits and passionate ways. The rain was like a wall around my world. It beat against my spirit and my brain, and I found myself spending more and more time doing nothing, living in daydreams and memory hours on end.

When Hamlet walked in through the door, my world would change. He brought back the light and spirit that somehow slipped through my grasp while he was away. We would talk and laugh, and I'd serve him a good, hot dinner. A joy so warm I could feel it would fold around me, and I'd think to myself—*tomorrow will be better. Tomorrow I won't be such a baby, I'll be all right*. But the next morning he would walk out the door and leave me with nothing but chilly, grey skies and empty hours. As soon as he closed the door I felt different inside; scared again, lonely, and withdrawn.

I didn't know how bad it was really getting until one day when Hamlet came in a little early. He looked around with his quick, appraising eye.

"This place is a mess, Ivy."

I looked up, startled. He had never spoken to me in that tone of voice before. He pulled off his boots and slicker and old, tweed jacket, and rubbed his beard as he looked about the place.

"Did you bake new bread today?" His voice was demanding.

"There's enough left over from yesterday," I said, surprised at the whiny defensiveness in my voice.

Hamlet stomped over to the pantry shelves and threw open the doors.

"Little more than a loaf end, stale at that. And not of yesterday's baking."

"I haven't felt well lately. You know that!"

"That's an excuse and *you* know it. You're well enough to keep up your regular chores."

"How do you know?" I screamed. "What do you know about me, anyway? Your cattle and your fields are more important than I am. I'm tired of—"

He didn't let me get any further. He made some kind of a sound deep down in his throat, grabbed my wrist so that his tightened fingers hurt.

"I'm tired of you feeling sorry for yourself." His voice was low and calculated, vibrating with the strength of emotions held in check. "I never expected self-pity from you, Ivy. Never."

I knew he was right, and because of that, more than anything, I couldn't bear it! I felt so small, so ashamed, so torn inside.

"You have no right to judge me! You don't understand!" I felt the tears at last spilling from my eyes.

He loosened his grip on my wrist—slowly—and backed away. There was a look in his eyes I had never expected to see. It wasn't anger or selfishness, but pain—pain and disappointment. I turned away, and in that instant he wheeled toward the door and was gone before I could cry out or call him back.

I flung myself on the big, feather bed in the corner and sobbed in utter abandon, my own pain eating a burning hole within my heart.

How could he ever trust or respect me again? What of the sweet spirit I'd promised to keep in my home?

I lay there, bitterly blaming my weakness and pride. Then, without warning, the pity would rise up in me: He *was* unkind. He didn't care what I was feeling. He wasn't a woman—pregnant, lonely, and scared. He didn't care. He didn't love me anymore!

I cried until I was exhausted, then sat up and blew my nose and dabbed cool water over my aching eyes. It was dark outside! A sharp fear began to clutch my middle. I ran to the window and peered into the gloom. Where was Hamlet? I couldn't see him anywhere! Then I drew back sharply as a small voice inside me whispered, *"Don't let him see you! Make him come in and apologize."*

So I waited in the dark and silent house, but he didn't come. I grew hungry, and then chilled, and with each passing minute my stomach tightened more; part of me terrified, part of me angry and hard.

I huddled on the bed and tried to sleep, ignoring the voice that urged me to light the fire, fix his supper, and go out to the barn and get him. At last I slept, but only fitfully; half-rising in my sleep a dozen times, aware that Hamlet wasn't there beside me.

When at first I swam into wakefulness the next morning, I couldn't recall what had happened, what was amiss. Cramped and stiff, I raised myself on one elbow. The hearth was cold, the sun-washed room stood empty and Hamlet's side of the bed had not been slept in all night. *How could he?* I felt a strange, affronted shame. He was trying to hurt me on purpose! Well, see if I cared! I'd never let him know it—never, never! I'd never give him further cause to despise me.

I rose quickly, ignoring the dull ache in my back, and the faintness that sometimes came when I didn't eat. Other pregnant women had borne worse than this! I dressed quickly and pulled my hair back from my face, then thought better and chose my prettiest apron to wear, combed my hair and carefully plaited it on my head. He'd be sorry he'd hurt me. I'd make him want me again—then *he* could feel what it was like to be rejected!

I built up the fire, mixed bread dough and put it aside, then stirred a batch of cornbread and set it frying. I had never moved so fast! I pulled back the bright, chintz curtains and scrubbed the window, then swept the floor with a passion and shook the rag rug. I kept watching for Hamlet, but even when I drew fresh water I didn't see him.

The cornbread sizzled and browned, but he didn't come. I set it aside to cool, milked the cow, fed the chickens, and gathered the morning eggs.

Ironically—perversely—the rain had stopped. A pale, autumn sun warmed the freshened valley. I churned the butter and cut up apples for a pie, then I tackled a bundle of mending I had ignored. The more I did, the better I felt inside. I cut up meat and vegetables for a stew and set it simmering far back on the fire.

Just in case, I kneaded the rising dough. There would be warm, brown bread for Hamlet. He hadn't eaten since yesterday noon.

I moved my rocking chair to the spot of sunlight which shimmered through my window and spread across the floor. I would work on the pair of stockings I was knitting.

I pulled my workbasket close and felt for the stockings. They weren't there. I must have tucked them away, thinking to keep them for a surprise. I pulled open the heavy, mahogany dresser—the bottom drawer where my own, special things were kept. I moved things about, looking for the stockings. I never found them. My eyes rested on the tidy, ribbon-tied package, at least a good inch thick, that contained all the letters Hamlet had ever written me—clear back to the first, rough, school-boy note he'd penciled.

Almost fearfully I drew them out, then sat cradling them in my lap while I rocked, back and forth, back and forth. I knew it would be dangerous for me to read them now, weaken my stubborn determination to nurse my anger. But I couldn't help myself. I drew one out.

Dear Ivy, I missed seeing you at school yesterday. Did you truly walk home with Mary and talk about me? Some "little girls" behave that way—but never you. Please do not forget to wait for me tomorrow. Yours forever, Hamlet.

I smiled at the dozens of memories his words revived. "Yours forever." How strange that he had written it that way. He *was* mine forever now, though neither of us had dreamed back then that such a thing could really happen.

I read another letter, then another. Each one thrust fingers of memory and love and pain into my heart. I opened one more. This he had written the day after I first agreed to become his wife. We were both in England then—a far, lost world—so innocent of all that lay ahead!

My dearest, I awoke this morning fearing last night was only a dream. How can one man be as happy as you have made me? I want to make you happy, Ivy, I do! But I know so little of women and their ways. At times it frightens me, for I never wish to hurt you or disappoint you...

My throat was beginning to ache with unshed tears. The bitterness of last night was slipping away. Vivid again was his love—and how much I loved him!

...but I shall be content to labour at it all my life. Learning how to love you and make you happy...

I couldn't bear it! I set the letters aside and hastily filled a small bucket with the hot stew, wrapped the warm bread in a towel, and filled an earthenware jug with the morning's new milk. I packed them in a basket, my fingers shaking, and fairly flew through the door in my eagerness.

I ran till my lungs were burning, and then I saw him. He was coming along the path from the farthest fields. I slowed to watch him; he hadn't noticed me yet. He bent down for a moment, and when he straightened he saw me. I held my breath and it seemed my heart would stop, afraid that he would turn away, but he didn't. He walked purposefully forward, and I saw that he carried flowers in his hand, a bunch of wild field flowers he had gathered for me.

With a cry, I dropped the basket and ran toward him. He took me into his arms and swung me round, then stopped and held me close and let me cry. His touch sent shivers through me—his fingers along my arm, caressing my hair, and the warmth of his body pressed against my own. I raised my face, though dreading to meet his eyes.

"Hamlet, please forgive me!" The words were a cry.

He cupped my chin with his hand. There were tears in his eyes.

"I was coming to ask your forgiveness," he began.

I broke away. "No, it's I who hurt you first. I saw it in your eyes. Oh, Hamlet, forgive me. I can't bear to think of you looking at me that way."

Then I noticed the ragged cut along his wrist.

"What's this?" I cried, fearfully taking his hand.

"My excuse," he replied without smiling.

"You'd hurt yourself—and I didn't even notice."

"Stop it, Ivy. I was feeling sorry for myself. That was the problem. I was so dog-tired—"

"And *hurt!*" I interrupted.

"It's little more than a scratch!" His voice was hard, but his eyes, in their pain and frustration, were little-boy eyes, and I sensed how desperately he had needed me—a woman's tender fussing and attention.

"I failed you," I said, my voice just above a whisper.

"No!" He took my shoulders and held me firmly. "I was blaming you for the very thing I was doing—feeling sorry for myself. The only difference was, you had a reason."

I stared at him, amazed. "Hamlet, that's not fair."

He placed his hand over the gentle swell of my stomach.

"You were right. I don't know what it's like for you. I promised to love and protect you and make you happy—"

"And you do, you do! I won't listen to any more."

I caught his face in my hands and kissed his lips. He laughed against my mouth, then kissed me back.

"That's the only way I've found to shut you up," I said at last.

He smiled, but didn't protest.

We spread the food out beneath a tree, sat on the gnarled roots, and ate together. It was one of the sweetest meals I have ever tasted, seasoned with peace, the high, sweet song of birds, and the singing of my own, grateful heart.

6

Courage and comfort!
All shall yet go well.
SHAKESPEARE

It was Thanksgiving, and Hamlet had promised a trip back to the fort! There was a thin feathering of brittle snow on the ground when we left, but the sun was warm and the journey not unpleasant.

November. The harvest was over, and it was truly a time of thanksgiving, a time for feeling a oneness with the land. So it was for me. I felt like the early pilgrims, Englishmen whose blood and sweat and tears had nurtured the soil that in turn had nurtured them when the cycle of giving and gathering had begun. On that Thanksgiving I was a little less a stranger: this was America—this was Zion—this was me.

When we reached the fort, I could scarcely wait to fly into Lydia's sturdy, waiting arms, happy to let her mother me again. There were so many friends to greet, so much news to exchange. That first night we talked till our tired brains stopped our tongues, and slept in the morning until we felt like waking.

To me, Phineas looked thin and a little more bent,

though he seemed as bright and spry as before. He was just as capable of getting into mischief! Some Indian had given him a long, feathered bonnet. It was his pride and joy and he refused to take it off. He would strut and prance and chant like the Indians did, and when things got slow, he loved to sneak up on people: old Sister Henniger hanging out her clothes, a group of small boys innocently fishing in the pond, and he had even snuck up on mothers exercising their babies.

Phineas could whoop in a way that made your insides curl and there had been angry complaints against him most every day, but no one could discover how to stop or even control him. Then one afternoon while we were there, he happened to pull his trick on the wrong person.

Parley Benson had a shock of bristly red hair, and a bristly temper to match it. That warm afternoon, he was sitting against a gate post cleaning his guns. There was a half-empty whiskey bottle propped up beside him, and two others, empty, rattling at his feet. He was singing to himself, enjoying the discord, and didn't hear a thing till the chilling whoop sounded within inches of his ear. He jumped with a screech of his own and grabbed the whiskey, as it was the closest thing at hand, and threw it at Phineas with a curse. Phineas, still dancing and whooping, happened to duck at the right time, so Parley grabbed a gun and threw that too. Phineas loved it and didn't have sense enough to get out of there. Finally, Parley, with hands and fingers shaking, found a gun that was loaded, swung it high with a grunt of satisfaction, and began to pepper the air with outraged shot.

Phineas owed his life to the empty bottles and the blinding temper. Skittering up and down like a Mexican jumping bean he somehow escaped each barking bullet that Parley sent, and those who happened to watch the performance swore that no Indian ever danced better! Phineas and his bonnet became immortal, and the fort was buzzing with talk of it for a long while.

*   *   *

40

"Have you felt the baby yet?" Lydia asked me one morning.

I admitted a little shyly that I had.

"It will seem more real to you every day," she promised. We talked then of babies and birthings and womanly things. I had never watched a baby being born. Lydia promised, when my time came in the spring, she would drive out and help me through the ordeal. I couldn't picture that moment as ever coming, picture the child within me as real and alive.

One morning while we were there the Indians came. I had almost forgotten my fear and my repulsion. The squaws, many with papooses bound to their backs, went from door to door begging biscuits, flour, sugar, or bread. What food they obtained was dropped into the long, dirty sacks they carried.

Their hair was dirty, their dresses black with grease and grime, and belted—always belted at the waist. From the belt hung chains and beaded ornaments, and small, sharp knives that clinked and jostled against them when they walked. I stared with fascination at those women, hunched beneath their long, loose shawls, and wondered at their inscrutable faces.

"Are you looking for your friend?" Lydia had come up behind me, her tone light and teasing. "He'll be along. He looks for you, too, you know."

"He doesn't!" I protested.

"Indeed he does. Asks about you every time he comes."

"But why?" I felt a coldness inside.

"Well, he took a fancy to you, hon. Besides, you made him a big man with his friends. A gift like that from a young, pretty, white squaw. He still struts around with that mirror—you ought to see it."

She laughed, just thinking about him, but I couldn't smile.

"Well, he may have thought I was pretty," I retorted,

"but he reserves most of his admiration for himself."

I saw him before he saw me, and I'll admit I nearly laughed at his proud, overbearing manner, and the exaggerated way he admired himself. One moment he spied me, and the next he was there at my side, his dark eyes filled with laughing admiration. I managed a smile and nodded my head a little.

He held the mirror out toward me until I could see my own face in the glass, then murmured something in admiration. I was embarrassed, and my face felt hot beneath his gaze. Yet that awful fear didn't burn and choke inside me and when at last I dared look up into his eyes, my embarrassment faded. I felt appreciative in a humble sort of way.

"Hel-lo," he said.

I stared a moment, not daring to laugh. His warm eyes were too serious and intent.

"Hello," I replied, and smiled with greater ease.

"Yan-no," he said, pointing grandly to himself.

"Ivy," I answered, touching my own arm. "Ivy."

"I-vy," he repeated. "I-vy. Ivy."

He held up the mirror before me and shook it a little.

"Yan-no say thank you. Thank you this, Ivy."

How carefully he sounded out the words.

"You are welcome," I said, smiling sincerely, and then pointed at the mirror. "Looking glass. Looking glass."

"Hum-pah?" He looked at it wonderingly. "Loo-king glass. Loo-king glass."

Then he pressed it against my fingers.

"Nah-voo," he said.

"Oh! Nah-voo," I repeated hesitantly.

He beamed, smiling with every muscle of his face.

"Nah-voo—looking glass," he repeated again.

I nodded. His wide smile broke. He grabbed my hand and shook it, then bounded away, muttering the strange, new syllables under his breath.

That hadn't been so awful, I thought, breathing one long sigh, *not at all. In fact—*

"So your fine, feathered friend found you!" said Lydia, coming up beside me.

"Yes, yes he did."

I followed her indoors while she chatted merrily about that and a dozen matters. But I was silent, busy with my own thoughts.

Only two weeks until Christmas. I couldn't believe it! I still had so much to do to make things just right. A dozen little surprises I had started and could only work on when Hamlet was out-of-doors. And then there was the baking and the cleaning.

A flurry of snowflakes blew against the pane. This was the first real storm of December. I untied my apron and stooped down to open the dresser. The thick snow would soon drive Hamlet indoors. I had better work on his shirt while I had a chance.

I moved to pull open the drawer, but cried out instead!

A sharp pain ran through me like the searing blade of a knife. With whitened hands, I clutched the edge of the wood. The pain eased a little, but when I tried to move, it struck me again and spread like a spreading fire. Something awful was happening to me, but what? I felt strong muscles inside me tighten and close. The baby! Oh no—please, no!

I struggled to rise. I must get help—I must somehow get to Hamlet! I pulled myself up, but the pain was awful now. I could hear myself whimpering somewhere far away. I moved—one step—two—then a weakness swept through me, a dizziness that made the whole room spin and reel. I clutched for the dresser, the bed—anything—but my frantic fingers found nothing but empty space, and the emptiness closed about me as I fell.

I don't remember anything that happened. I never saw

43

the child. I never gazed at the lifeless little face. I was somewhere off in a fog I couldn't fight through. Lydia came and stayed till the worst was over, fed me gallons of sassafras tea to thicken the blood, ergot to stem the hemorrhage, and laudanum to relieve some of the pain.

I didn't feel the pain or her gentle fingers, nor hear her friendly chatter and Hamlet's low pleas. I was off somewhere, and neither of them could reach me. I remember once or twice the fear in their eyes as their faces swam into my view, then dissolved again. I remember hearing someone softly crying, but not till much later did I know that the cries had been my own.

Then one day I opened my eyes and it was over. I was there again—I could see, and I could feel. And then the pain began in deadly earnest. But I chose to ignore the pain, to drive it away. I smiled with a stony face. I let them help me. I swallowed the tea and ate the thick, warm gruel, and took the medicines that Lydia gave me. I did everything they asked me to do but talk. I couldn't talk, and finally they stopped trying.

When Lydia left I thought it might be better, but it was worse, much worse with just Hamlet and me alone. He paced the house like a caged and cornered wild thing. I watched him—till his darkened eyes turned on me. I couldn't bear to meet those suffering eyes.

It wasn't something purposeful I did. I had swum out of the fog, but not the weakness, and the weakness had a hold on my brain as well. I couldn't cry or scream, I couldn't fight it. I was helpless to do more than hang onto life, existing somewhere on the surface of what I had been.

On Christmas Day, I was strong enough to get up, walk a little, and sit in my chair by the hearth. Hamlet tried—how pathetically hard he tried. It made me ache inside just watching him. He brought me good, warm food to eat by the fire, and surprised me with little presents he'd made for the day. He fought back his own lonely pain and tried hard to please me. Part of me cried for him, but part of me stood detached, unmoved, impersonal, and uninvolved.

Hours had passed, the day was slipping by us. I don't think Hamlet could bear it any more. He moved my chair so that I faced him, then held my chin so I couldn't turn away.

"I can't live like this," he said, his voice sounding hollow.

The music . . . it's left his voice, I thought—and the thought caused me pain.

"It's that simple," he continued. "You have to help me."

He paused, and I saw the tears gathering in his eyes. Something deep within me stirred, then fluttered.

"I can't help you like this! We're dead to each other, Ivy!"

His voice held a note of panic, shrill and high. I wanted to help him, but something was choking me, choking the fluttering warmth his words had stirred. He took both my hands, his own hands warm and demanding.

"Come back, come back!"

The words were a desperate whisper. I felt something fold up and crumple inside me.

"It's Christmas, Ivy. Please give yourself back to me!"

Something of what I was feeling must have shown in my face: the fear, the searing pain, the joy of release! He opened his arms and his eyes became alive.

"HAMLET!" I screamed his name with a thousand voices—all the voices which had held me mute before. It was the highest and the lowest, both together. It was heaven and hell. It was all that I could bear!

And through it all Hamlet held me, tirelessly. And in the end, when everything else had perished, his love remained, his power, and the heaven of knowing that his love would never die.

7

The icy fang—
And churlish chiding of the
winter's wind.

SHAKESPEARE

The long, cold winter closed upon us, blanketed us with silence and snow. Ours was a constant battle with the elements; no friendly forces now, but set against us. The heavy snows, the icy, chilling winds: how quickly they could strike, destroy, pass on. Hamlet fought—repairing fences, nursing stock, chopping through thick ice to where the water still ran. We husbanded the wood, the food, the light. Never, in all those long months, was I ever thoroughly warm.

For me, part of the struggle was in having too much time to think. I fought against the dragging weight of depression, the comfort of self-pity. Not again! But what I hated most was feeling a stranger once more. I couldn't overcome the deep conviction that something in this land had betrayed me and didn't care: we could leave tomorrow and the land would only be glad.

"You see," the wind would whisper, "we drove them away." The snow would sigh and drift over our scars on the land and cover all traces that proved we had ever existed.

I tried to keep busy. When there was nothing to do I

took up my sewing, until my thoughts drove me from it. I would read and re-read the few books we had, until restlessness drove me from that. Then I'd scour the kettle or re-arrange my shelves for the hundredth time. If I worked at it, I reasoned, I could defeat the threatening depression.

At times I found I was actually singing to myself, and I know it pleased Hamlet to hear me when he came in. At other times I would sit at the wooden table and run my fingers back and forth across it, pretending the piano keys were there. I would "practice" every piece I knew over and over, remembering in my mind the rhythm and feel as well as the arrangement of the keys. If I forgot a piece my mind would begin to panic. I mustn't forget! Someday there would be a piano, and little fingers needing to be taught.

Music. My children would not grow up without music!

My children! There was no music ... there were no children now.

The best times were the long, grey afternoons when Hamlet was indoors with me! How could gloom survive against his smile? We never had to wonder what to do. He invented simple games for us to play, we read and sang, and he helped me card and spin. We roasted nuts or popped corn in the fire. I would sit and embroider while he would mend harnass leather, or merely whittle, amusing me with stories and tall tales. He was the very light of my existence. And, bit by bit, his strong insistent light began to spark and build my own weak flame. Bit by bit the warmth returned inside me.

We talked of many things, but not the child. The child that should have been, that was no more. Each long, winter day that broke upon me, grey and hostile, was an enemy I must outface, must set myself against. I refused to be defeated by all the enemies the grey hours held. One more day of living through the hours—then Hamlet came, and I was whole again. Day by day the fight became less bitter, and there came a day when I knew the wholeness would win.

It was good I had grown stronger before that night. The night when the white peace shattered about my feet. We were sound asleep, cuddled close against each other. We heard the sharp sound, hollow against the dark. The cracking of wood, the shot, the muffled cry.

Hamlet was up and out before I was half-dressed, his long, old Hawken absent from its place. I fought the panic within me, the strangling fingers of fear. I grabbed my heaviest shawl, my fingers fumbling, but paused at the door—at the onslaught of cold and blackness that struck my face.

I strained, but heard nothing. Was Hamlet in the barn? My knees felt weak, my heart was pumping madly, my imagination torturing my fears. Then I heard him, ever so faintly.

"It's all right, Ivy. I'm in here."

I followed his voice, then the sudden light of a lantern, and entered the musty barn, shivering and tense.

Hamlet stood holding the lantern, his fair hair tousled, the line of his eyebrows knit in a troubled frown. He looked so young, so vulnerable there. Then I noticed the trail of blood through the matted straw, and out and into the snow.

"One of the cows. The buff one, with the white star."

"Oh, Hamlet!"

"They rifled the smokehouse too." He moved and I followed, held up my skirts and struggled through the wet snow.

It was true. The lock had been sprung and the door left open. Apples and crushed potatoes littered the floor. Most of the meat was gone, though sausages still hung in the rafters, along with a small side of ham high out of reach. The barrels of vegetables were tipped and rolled over, and what had not been taken lay smashed and ruined at our feet.

"Indians?" The unanswered question hung in the air. Hamlet struck his cold hands angrily together.

"Must have been. Well ... they need it more than we do."

"Hamlet!" My blood was boiling. "That's fine to say. Next time it will be us as well as the cow."

He looked at me in his quiet, searching way.

"You can't just leave it, Hamlet."

"Well, what can I do? What do you propose, Ivy?" He spread out his hands. "Do you want me to go out there, try tracking them down?"

"No—no!" I recoiled against the preposterousness of that. "I just feel so trapped—so helpless! And so afraid."

He touched my hair with a sudden, tender gesture.

"They were hungry, Ivy, that's all. Go on inside, you're freezing to death out here. I'll clean up this mess."

I hesitated.

"Go on now," he said, smiling a little. I turned and did what he said.

The house was cold, but it would be wasteful to start a fire. I hugged my knees against me under the quilt and sat there, trembling, waiting for his return. I shook with more than cold. I was angry inside.

I had left my fear of Indians at the fort. I didn't want them intruding here as well. Was there nowhere their dark, beady eyes didn't penetrate? Of course they knew we were here! How foolish I'd been—to think we were safe and unnoticed—hidden, somehow. I could imagine them watching us now from some lofty vantage, laying cold, ruthless plans about how they meant to destroy us.

The snow and the wind and the cold were our enemies; silent, powerful, and impersonal. But now there were dark shadows out in the snow. And the shadows had flesh and substance, brain and breath. The shadows were a much more treacherous enemy. They wouldn't melt or soften with the spring. They would always be there watching us, waiting for their chance to strike again.

With early spring came terrible floods—filthy, brown water that widened the thin stream beds, uprooted trees, and carried the bloated carcases of cattle, with glazed and frozen eyes, along in the torrent. The floods swept the dams away just when the water was needed, and our tired hands had to build and rebuild again.

Early spring also brought the wildflowers that covered the fields in a dozen, bright patterns. There were sun birds and song birds, and new, spindly-legged calves. No matter what the trials, we could bear them. It was spring—and there was promise in the air.

I hovered over my peach shoots and my roses, tending them as carefully as I knew how. My need for them to live went very deep. I tried to tell myself it didn't matter; I had lost more important things than that. But loss isn't something the young can accept with ease. To fight against it was healthy; to fight was life.

There were days that spring when the beauty and joy seemed to blend and catch us into a shimmering, magical web. Hamlet and I behaved like lovers. We wandered through the fields gathering flowers, skipping like children, and kissing beneath the trees. We sang at the top of our lungs and laughed at nothing and ran through the rain barefooted till we were soaked. There was a sense of excitement just touching each other again; a catch in my breath when I looked at his fair, lean face, his warm eyes lingering on me, his wheat-gold hair.

There was no society here, no rules of decorum, no neighbors to lift their eyebrows or wag their heads. We lived in a world of our own—of our own making, and suddenly it was magic once again. Our love was tender and fluid, and filled with discovery. There were nights we would lie together beneath the stars, holding each other, part of the wonder we felt as we gazed at the worlds that stretched and spanned above us. The mountains, our only neighbors, our silent protectors, stood out in shapes of darkness against the night, bulwarks of solidarity, massive and still. One night I rested quietly against Hamlet, thinking, remembering back to the beginning.

"Something's going on in that head of yours," he said.

I could tell by the tone of his voice that he wouldn't ask, though he wanted me to tell him. He was a little more careful of me after what had happened in December. I took his hand and held it between mine.

"I was just remembering how I felt the day we were married."

He sat up a little.

"What, Ivy? What exactly?"

"Nothing really. Just being aware of how little we really knew each other, and how much that would change."

"I wondered about that too."

"You did?"

"Oh, yes. I couldn't imagine what it would be like to be part of another person—and that other person a woman, as well."

"You make 'woman' sound like some kind of strange creature."

"Well?" he retorted, his eyebrows raised quizically.

I laughed and he laughed, and my love for him flowed through my veins.

"In less than a year, Hamlet, we've shared more than I thought we would share in a lifetime. Does that sound silly?"

"No." He stroked my hair somewhat absently. "You've suffered more than I ever meant you to suffer."

He said it softly, tensing against my reaction. I looked into his wonderful eyes.

"*We've* suffered," I said.

Something more sprang into his gaze when I said the words. We looked deep into each other, not needing the crutch of speaking any more. A singular impression struck me then. It was very much like looking into the mirror—the gilt-framed, Wesley mirror where I had seen past myself to those who were part of me. His face was familiar, it fit, it was part of the image.

8

In such a night as this,
When the sweet wind did gently kiss
the trees.

SHAKESPEARE

One morning Hamlet rose before sunrise and rode to the fort at Hobble Creek to purchase some new stock. Slowly he was building a little herd. He liked the cattle better than the sheep, though he kept a few for the sake of wool and mutton. I preferred the more gentle sheep over cattle, myself. But as the hours passed, I grew excited, anxious to see the animals Hamlet would bring.

I heard his little entourage before I saw it, and ran out to welcome the newcomers home. There were six new animals, all looking very much like one another, but silky, fat, and healthy. There was Prudence, the draft mare Hamlet had ridden, but where was Hamlet? Prudence was running loose among the bulky cattle, and Hamlet wasn't on her back. Then I saw him, and caught in my breath at the sight.

He was riding a spotted, Indian pony that stretched its neck and pranced high as it stepped, seeming to sense that it was being watched and admired. The horse was beautiful to look at, and so was Hamlet, sitting astride the animal, tall and at ease, leaning a little forward to watch for me. I called out loudly and the horse skittered a little, but kept its stride. Hamlet slowed the horse down until I could come up beside him.

"Where did you find him?"

"Isn't he a beauty?" Hamlet's blue eyes were sparkling.

I nodded and touched the horse with a tentative hand. He stopped the animal and leaned out over the pommel.

"You won't believe it, Ivy." His voice was laughing with unmistakable boyish pride. "This crazy Navajo took a liking to your blanket."

"My blue star quilt?"

He nodded sheepishly.

"You were supposed to trade that with the eggs for things I needed—sugar and thread and needles—"

"I've got those things."

"But how? How could you?" I was suspicious, but his eyes were still dancing.

"I bought one less cow than I'd planned to. That was all."

"What else did you give for the pony?"

"Just—old Chewy."

"Chewy!"

Chewy was a burro we had inherited, thrown in with the first group of stock Hamlet bought. He was old and slow and very onery—little more than another mouth to feed.

"Well, I hope they don't eat him, Hamlet!"

"Your quilt would make a more tender meal than old Chewy."

We couldn't help laughing together at the idea, though we knew the possibility was real. The first Indian pony purchased in Pacen had been traded for an old ox that the Indian then turned around and ate. I only hoped they learned their lesson with the ox.

While Hamlet fed and watered the stock, I tried to make friends with the horse, though I was more shy of him than he was of me. He seemed gentle, with fine, quiet eyes. I knew the Navajos traded in fine horses, and could gentle a horse in their own secret ways. This one must have been broken carefully.

"What's his name?" I called across to where Hamlet was working.

"Te-ah. It's the Ute word for deer. Do you like it?"

"Te-ah. Yes. It fits him, don't you think?"

Having the horse worked wonders for Hamlet. Many of his tasks he was able to do now in half the time. He and the animal worked well together, and I enjoyed watching them move gracefully about the place.

In spite of Hamlet's urgings though, I wouldn't try riding. I had fallen from a horse when a little girl and broken my leg, and been left with a dread, an unreasoning fear. Since that time I had never sat on a horse again.

"Later," I promised. "Let me get used to him first." But time didn't serve to further my confidence.

Then one morning I went out as usual to gather the eggs and there, not yards from the house, sprung out of nowhere, stood a group of Indians—warriors and squaws. I drew in my breath, and felt the old fear clutch at me. What were they doing here? What did they want?

I edged back toward the door of the cabin. I could bolt the door, and hope that Hamlet would see them. He wasn't far, just out at the barn with his cows. If I refused to open the door, would they go away?

Then, out of the group of similar, unsmiling faces, one face detached itself, one lithe, sure frame, the head thrown back, a haughty, graceful manner—Yan-no!

A wave of relief surged over me.

He saw the recognition on my face, smiled, and bounded up beside me. I smiled; it was impossible not to. Was I really glad to see him?

"We going to fort," he said, in his practiced tones. "Stop

55

here. Say hello."

"Why, thank you, Yanno. That was very thoughtful."
He watched me carefully, then sighed, as though
content with my reply.

"Now," he declared in a tone of relieved dismissal, then
puffed out his chest in his usual haughty manner. "Now we
see Tow-ats-en—child."

He beamed, but something inside me drew tight and
cold. *No, please no*, I prayed silently. *I can't go through this. I can't!
I can't!*

His face looked puzzled and distressed when I failed to
answer.

"Tow-ats-en?" he said again, in quiet question.

I shook my head. I could feel the tears in my eyes.

"No Tow-ats-en," I said. "Tow-ats-en—child—is—dead.'

In any tongue, that was the first time I'd ever said it.

I didn't expect the pain that came over his features. He
dropped his eyes and mutterd under his breath.

"E-i," he said, and the sound became a wail.

E-i was the Ute word for dead. I shuddered, but he
raised his eyes to seek me, and I found that I could meet his
steady gaze.

"Yan-no understand. Yan-no—sorry—"

I took the hand he extended and found I was clutching it
hard.

"Thank you," I replied, but the words were barely a
whisper.

I hadn't heard Hamlet approaching, and neither had
Yanno, but suddenly I heard the horse and turned to see my
proud, young husband leading out his prize. Yanno whistled
appreciatively under his breath.

"A pretty nice piece of horseflesh, isn't he?" said
Hamlet.

Yanno nodded, and the two walked off together.
Hamlet stood head and shoulders above the Indian, but he
moved with as much fluidity and grace. I followed, lulled by

the pleasant sound of their voices, feeling serene inside, though not knowing why.

"I'm afraid not," I heard Hamlet say, and his voice was laughing. "Wild elephants couldn't get her up on that horse."

I flushed. Then Hamlet knew how afraid I was! I didn't hear Yanno's reply, but Hamlet nodded.

"Be my guest," he said, and held out the dangling reins. *He's letting Yanno ride the horse. That's nice—that's like Hamlet.* So I thought—unthreatened, innocently. Then Yanno was by my side, smiling widely and leading the pony quietly along.

I didn't understand till it was too late. His strong hands closed securely round my waist, and lifted me. I didn't have time to struggle. Suddenly I was sitting up in the air, feeling the smooth, warm horseflesh beneath my legs.

"No!" I clutched wildly for something to hold onto. "No! Hamlet, please make him stop!"

I was terrified. In a moment more I would scream and disgrace myself.

Then, with a swish, the Indian landed behind me, lightly—more poised than sitting. He drew up the reins and dug his bare knees into the pony's flanks, and the horse moved out. I could feel him gathering his strength beneath me. Hamlet and the cabin were soon left behind. In seconds, it seemed, we had passed the barn and the sheds. The wind began to curl itself through my hair. A sensation of pure excitement tingled over me—a freedom of body and spirit I'd never known. I leaned into the wind, and Yanno leaned with me. *He won't let anything hurt me,* I told myself.

"Poon-e-kee! Poon-e-kee!" he cried.

Look! he was saying.

I looked and saw three brilliant pheasants, startled by the horse, rise into the air, affronting the pale sky with their staining colors. I drank in their beauty, and then we passed them by, gathered more speed, and flew and flew and flew! I

57

closed my eyes, I never wanted to stop. Some joy, free from restraint, surged through my being. I felt light and graceful, powerful and free!

At some point, Yanno turned and we headed back. If I had known the words, I would have protested. As he drew in the horse and slowed us, my joy wound down and the magic dissolved—I couldn't prevent it. There was Hamlet, his face not quite in focus. At first, I didn't realize we had stopped. Yanno slid down and pulled me down beside him. My legs felt weak, almost numb.

"Hamlet," I cried.

He was there, and I leaned against him gratefully. I laughed, with all the joy that was left inside me.

"I loved it, Hamlet! I loved it!"

"Thank you, thank you!" I cried, turning to Yanno, and hoping he could feel what I wanted to say.

When he left with his friends, I turned again to Hamlet.

"Your eyes are still on fire," he said with a smile.

"Will you take me again?" I asked him.

"Good heavens, Ivy. You've a wild streak in your nature after all."

"Stop teasing me, Hamlet. I don't believe I can help it. It's like something new was born in me out there in the wind."

"Tonight," he promised, locking his arms around me. "We'll ride with the wind across the face of the moon."

I shivered.

"Will you hold me like this, Hamlet?"

He tightened his arms.

"With pleasure, my love, with pleasure."

He kept his promise. We rode the night wind together and whispered secrets only the stars could hear. I was not unaware that an Indian and an Indian pony had opened a world of wonder for me to tread, a wonder meant for Hamlet and me to share. It didn't seem incongruous to me. We were part of their world—and they were part of ours.

* * *

I waited until there couldn't be any mistake. But even then it was difficult to believe. I was going to have a baby again! I wavered between terror and joy. If I admitted, even to myself, how badly I wanted this baby, then I admitted pain too awesome for me to bear. Could I stand to lose this child as I lost the other?

When I told Hamlet, he couldn't keep the joy from his eyes.

"Things will be all right this time, Ivy. I know it."

I let him believe, but I didn't share his faith. I did, however, take special care of myself. No sudden bending, no pushing, no heavy lifting, no trips to Pacen, and no moonlight rides. I sacrificed those rides with a sense of resentment. They were magic, they were romance—they took me out of my world and lifted me to a taste of freedom and peace and power. Now everything in my life seemed dull and tasteless. I couldn't go anywhere or see anyone, or do a thing that captured my interest and heart. And all for what? For a false, unfounded hope? For something I couldn't see, something that would never become a reality?

I found myself longing for Jane, missing her terribly—her face, her manner of talking, her country ways. She was home, she was mother love, she was memory. Sometimes when Hamlet was gone I allowed myself to cry. Curled on the bed like a child, I would cry for my mother. I felt so young, so abandoned by the world. No one cared or knew what I had to face. And when I suffered, that too was mine alone.

One Sunday afternoon we sat reading together, Hamlet the Book of Mormon and I the Bible. I was sleepy and the pages of Exodus couldn't hold me. My mind kept wandering to my own, vast exodus—away from home, away from my own land—my people, my customs, my ways. Everything about my life was new: the food, the way of speech and dress—the country, the lifestyle, the religion. Which of it was me and which was only an uncomfortable shape I'd fit myself into? How could the many shapes and pictures mould, form into a strong and sensible whole?

Hamlet closed his book and set it down beside him.

"I'd like to give you a blessing, Ivy," he said.

I came quickly back to the moment and his words.

"You do? Are you sure?"

I had never had a blessing, though I'd seen ever so many administered to on the trek. I held a firm belief in the priesthood power. I had not only seen it work, but had felt it there too many times to doubt what it could do.

He came over to me and knelt beside my chair and took my hands in his before he answered.

"These weeks since you told me I've been praying a lot," he confided. "I feel now I can bless you as I ought to—with power, with confirmation of the spirit."

So I sat in my own chair as he placed his hands upon my head. He spoke with quiet sureness, and his words seemed to spring from some source of power I could actually feel. I listened, and I felt a warmth flow through me, a quiet peace—if peace can be the word—because the peace thrilled like a warming flame. He finished, and I knew his words were truth.

"You shall bear children," he had told me firmly, "come through your trials, and know the greatest joys of motherhood here upon the earth. And you shall know the hand of the Lord is with you."

His words were enough.

I stood.

His eyes were tear-filled like my own. Something deep, eternal moved between us, much as it had the day when we were sealed. He had brought it, with his priesthood and his love.

9

To make a virtue of necessity,
And live, as we do, in this wilderness.

SHAKESPEARE

I looked out and saw the gathering cloud of dust. Then, straining, I discerned the shapes of copper bodies, and shiny, black heads that glistened in the sun. Indians! Yanno must be coming!

The heat of June was shimmering, breathless. I ventured outside as little as I could and this was just what I needed to pull me out of my lethargy. I hastily finished the work I was doing and set the stew far back on the fire. The little group was closer now. Some of the men rode horses—and there were children.

I ran outside. The air seemed to throb and rise in waves that rippled on and on. I shaded my eyes with my hand. Where was Yanno? I couldn't pick him out from among the braves. The cold feeling I had almost forgotten crept into my stomach. There were no faces I recognized here. Who were these people? What could they want from me?

I stood with my face a mask, like their faces, my back held straight, my head thrown high. Why was Hamlet always gone at times like this? They drew close and one, a spokesman, pulled out from the others. I waited for him to approach me and didn't speak. But what I saw sent shivers along my spine.

The children with the group were Indian slave children, most probably stolen from some enemy tribe. Miserable little creatures, they barely looked human. I dug my fingernails hard into my palm.

The three little faces before me were smeared with blood and dirt, and gaunt with hunger. Their hair had been shingled with butcher knives and fire, but that wasn't the worst that the fire brands had done.

Their captors had hacked the fleshy parts of their bodies with knives, then stuck live fire brands into the wounds. The thin little bodies were caked with blood and ashes. I clenched my teeth; I felt that I might be sick. A fire of anger and pain welled up within me. I wanted to spit at the face that was watching mine. I wanted to torture him as he'd tortured those children.

"You want?" he said, in sloppy, gutteral tones. "Sell— cheap."

He reached back and pulled one of the captives forward. The little girl was six, perhaps seven years old. She stared straight ahead, her dark eyes wide and blank.

Could I buy this child? If only Hamlet were here! To buy her, I knew, might very well save her life. I had heard the stories of Wanship and Walker and others. Without care, the child might easily starve to death, or, if she angered her captors, have her brains dashed out on a rock. Her life to them meant less than nothing at all. Quickly I calculated what I might give.

"Wait," I cried, and ran quickly back into the house, snatching all I dared trade without Hamlet's permission. I set it in a bundle before the chief: bright beads, a little mirror such as I'd given Yanno, a piece of yard goods I had meant to make into a dress, and the last of the sugar Hamlet had brought home with the pony.

The man made a snorting noise far back in his throat.

"Guns," he said, in a voice filled with disdain. "These squaw goods—we want guns—weapons."

My heart trembled within me! I had no guns. I couldn't give them any of Hamlet's pieces; he had no more than he needed himself.

I stole a glance at the girl. She stood still and listless, but suddenly her eyes moved and looked at me. I smiled, my tenderness bare upon my face. I shall never forget the tiny, golden spark that came to life behind her empty gaze.

Bullets! I could try bullets—perhaps a knife. I held out my hand and fled back inside once again. I took as many bullets as I dared, emptied them into my apron, then grabbed a knife, and yet another, hoping Hamlet could get more at the fort. I ran back outside and emptied them on the ground with the other goods.

"All of this," I said, sweeping my arm.

He shook his head and spat on the ground beside him.

I felt my nails dig deep into my flesh. Without allowing myself to think of the consequences, I turned and entered the house, breathless now, and grabbed the slender Hawken from its place. One gun—just one—one gun for one small life.

I walked with what forced dignity I could muster, thrust the gun forward, and held it before the chief. While he handled it and looked it over, my heart stood still. There was a painful throbbing way in the back of my throat.

He handed it back to me and turned aside.

"No good," he said, and bent to pick up the rope that was tied about the neck of the little girl.

"Please!" I cried, but he didn't even look back.

"We get better price at fort."

The group began to move with much muttering. He kicked the youngest child where he sat in a heap.

"One-e—meah-bikeway."

Stand up! Move! he was telling them. They moved, and the little girl didn't even look back.

I stumbled into the house and sank down on the floor. How long I huddled there I don't know, but I was still sobbing when Hamlet came in at sunset, and even his tender arms couldn't stop the tears.

The heat was unbearable, but the dust was worse. And beyond the torment of dust, there were the insects. The dry heat seemed to make them breed by the thousands; dozens of strange new bugs that had no names, but worked their silent destruction and then moved on. We lost whole sections of fields to fly maggots, and more to the crawling crickets, which came and settled over the fields like a black blanket. It was such a gruesome job to clear them out. Nothing worked but burying them or burning, and the stench that rose with the smoke and hung on the air was sickly sweet and churned inside me for days.

I found the loathsome creatures in my cupboards, trapped in a glass, or crawling across my bread. Every crack and crevice would fill with their bodies, or they would fall into the water and float there, dead. We shook them out of the quilt at bedtime, and even found them tangled and caught in my hair! Then I would scream and scream, but it did no good. I lived for days with the sensation of something crawling—along the hairs on my arm, at the back of my neck—and found myself swatting and scratching and brushing at nothing. The crawling sensation nearly drove me mad.

I had never seen Hamlet so close to discouragement before. We were losing so much that had come to us so hard won. He fell asleep before he could eat his food. His hands were cut and scorched and tender, and his face grew almost gaunt—the fair skin burned.

The peach trees were only sticks, there was little to eat there, but one day I noticed the leaves on the rosebushes turning brown. I couldn't tell what it was, I could only tend them, and worry and fuss and pray. In the end, the brown spread, with little yellow spots in it, eaten through by some small, crawling thing. Soon there was more yellow than green. Then there was no green at all, and I had lost another battle!

I walked alone that night while Hamlet slept. *If I made a list,* I told myself angrily, *on one side recording things gained, on the other, things lost, there wouldn't be much of a contest.* What *had* I gained? Experience in suffering, little more. Every inch of progress came through struggle, but even then there were no guarantees. We were just as likely to lose it all again! It wasn't fair! Bitterly I thought of Salt Lake City. The Saints there weren't struggling like this. What was the purpose of it? Oh, why did Hamlet want this kind of life?

For the first time since my marriage I felt a schism, an alienation between his spirit and mine. It was his fault I was suffering here! *Oh, mother, where are you?* I cried into the darkness. *Why did you bring me here, then leave me alone? I need you—I need you!*

But there was no voice to answer, no feeling but the aching of my own heart.

There was no wind to blow away the insects, no moisture to wet the dry, cracked earth. Hamlet irrigated as much as he could, and carried the water by hand—when there was water. But finally the stream became a trickle, then the trickle dried to moistened, marshy spots, good for breeding maggots and mosquitoes.

One morning Hamlet sat longer than usual over his breakfast. It frightened me how bleary-eyed he looked; exhausted after sleeping all night.

"I need to find some water," he said.

I knew he was right. Our supply was nearly depleted. We had enough for four, maybe five days longer—water to keep the animals alive, a little for ourselves. When that was gone?

"Where will you go?" How calm my voice sounded!

Where will you go? I had asked instead of crying, *Hamlet, please don't leave me! I'm frightened! What will I do without you? What if the Indians come? What if something happens with the baby? What if you don't find water at all? What if you don't come back again?*

He raised his eyes slowly. Seeing them, I didn't need to speak. All my tortured questions crowded there.

"I'll try Walker's Flat first, then go further up if I have to."

I nodded. At Walker's Flat there were springs of fresh, mountain water. He could load the wagon with barrels and fill them there.

"You're leaving now?"

It was his turn to nod.

I cooked and packed his food while he prepared for the journey.

Just before leaving, he lifted the Hawken down.

"You remember how to use this?"

I nodded, but my face apparently didn't convince him.

"Let me show you," he said, and patiently took me over each step again, until he was certain I wouldn't make a mistake.

"Ivy, remember, don't hesitate to use this—if you hear anything suspicious. Understand?"

I walked him to the wagon. We both just stood there.

"Two to four days. Don't worry till four days, Ivy." He squinted his eyes and looked at me quizically. "There's one thing you've forgotten," he said.

"What?" My mind searched frantically back over every item.

"This," he answered, pulling me into his arms and kissing me with a passion I hadn't expected—insistent, demanding—until he felt me respond.

At last, I drew away from him, breathless.

"That's more like it." The laughter was back in his voice. "That's a thing a girl can't afford to forget how to do."

I smiled. I couldn't help it. I wanted to cry at the joy that little smile brought into his eyes.

"Let's try once more," I suggested. "I want to make sure I've got it."

He kissed me again and I thought, as he held me, *I could stay in your arms forever like this!*

I didn't wait to watch him leave. I couldn't stand to see him grow more distant, and at last disappear. I walked resolutely indoors and did my dishes, cleaned up from the cooking, and straightened the room. I moved with determination, but slowly. All through that day, at every task, I slowed the pace as much as I could. The longer I was busy, the better. I dreaded empty, silent hours alone.

Night drew down around me. A dozen times I chided myself for being a baby, but the darkness seemed to unleash my nameless fears. Even kneeling to say my prayers I had to fight the urge to turn around and face whatever presence might be there. At last, throwing prudence to the wind, I lit a lamp and kept it burning. I heaped the cozy quilt around me, and read the Book of Mormon until I nodded, then actually sang myself to sleep with hymns.

It wasn't quite so bad the next night, but by the third night I was getting touchy, worn out with the pressure of facing life alone. There was absolutely no one but me. When I spoke, only the hot wind answered, moaning mysterious fears into my head. I found I was talking to the animals as I tended them—sometimes even talking to myself. It was such a struggle to keep up my spirits!

That night it took me much too long to fall asleep, but when I woke, I woke in one, quick instant and knew as quickly that it still was night, that something had awakened me!

Every muscle in my body froze. I listened—all my senses on edge.

The sound of footsteps.

I clutched the covers till my fingers ached. My mind was on fire, unable to think.

Silence.

Then the sound.

Was it nearer? I moved. The rope springs creaked beneath me, loud as a rifle crack in the silent room. My heart caught in my throat, but I kept on moving. It took a lifetime just to cross the room.

I lifted down the loaded Hawken.

Where was the noise?

I listened again. This time it was definitely closer.

Footsteps ... and a fumbling at the door! I stifled a pulsing urge to scream, caught my breath, and clenched the rifle. *Please, please go away. Please don't be real. Oh, please don't come in and hurt me!*

I wanted to scream and cry and whimper. Instead I stood and pointed the Hawken, waiting for the noise to come again. I said a dozen prayers in those few seconds, and Hamlet's words echoed in my mind. "Don't hesitate to use this."

Don't hesitate. That's just what I was doing! Slowly I pulled back the hammer and slid my finger over the trigger. When the noise came again, I would fire.

The door frame rattled.

I must shoot! But where? There by the latch, or square through the door's middle? Somewhere—I mustn't *hesitate!* My finger had already begun to squeeze the trigger, but I jerked as the rifle fired and missed the door by scanty inches.

"Ivy!"

Whoever was out there had called my name! My spine crawled with mingled fear and excitement. Should I call back? My fingers began to shake.

"Ivy!" said the voice again.

"HAMLET!"

"Yes. It's me."

I flew to unbolt the door. I laughed and cried and asked a hundred questions, till he had to shake me to get me to hold still.

"I could have killed you! I could have killed you!" I kept repeating. "Why did you come in the night? What if I'd shot you?"

Hamlet moved toward the fireplace before he began to talk, and I saw he was cutting bandages and stirring the embers to warm water there.

I found water at Walker's Flat late the first day," he told me. "I would have been home much sooner, but Prudence stumbled in a pothole and gashed her leg. It's pretty bad. I finally had to unyoke her. Jock's been pulling the load alone. Prudence and I walked a long way together."

"You scared me, Ivy," he admitted at last, pushing back his dampened hair and managing a grin.

"I'm sorry I had to frighten you. I thought I could call and alert you that way. I never thought you'd be so touchy that you'd be waiting with that old gun to blow my head off."

"Hamlet!"

He laughed, then turned to pour the water.

"Most of the barrels I unloaded a mile or two back. We can go tomorrow and pick them up. Let poor little Jock-o have a rest first."

I helped him carry the things out to the barn, and sat with him as he worked over Prudence, helping him a little here and there. I couldn't stop shivering, and my eyes were so tired they burned, but I didn't care. It was wonderful being with him—watching him, touching him, hearing the sound of his voice. He was here again, and everything was all right.

At last he stood, straightened, then arched his tired back.

"That ought to do it," he said with satisfaction.

"There's one thing you forgot."

"What's that?" he said, but it didn't take him long.

His weary eyes brightened as I went into his willing

arms. After long, delicious moments he drew back, grinning.

"You haven't forgotten a thing, my girl," he teased. "Yes ma'am, you do that very well."

Suddenly I wasn't tired. I moved into his arms again.

10

Of all the joys that lighten suffering earth,
What joy is welcomed like a new-born child?

SHAKESPEARE

Somehow the torment of summer spun out and ended, and autumn was here again. And somehow the child still lived and grew within me. The days were bearable now, even pleasant, with that sense of the purpose of things which harvest time brings.

I practiced my "piano" across the table and even began to sew a few things for the baby. I bottled vegetables for use in the winter, but Hamlet wouldn't let me overdo. Yet he could have used my hands and a dozen more.

He'd gone to Pacen once that summer, and yet again he had gone and returned with news. *This too,* I told myself, *will pass. There will be other years, other trips to Pacen. When I hold my child in my arms it will all be worth it.*

Lydia sent homemade preserves and a little note: "See you in December, darling. This time we'll make it work!"

I smiled and tucked the note in with my sewing, then sat with Hamlet while he talked and ate.

"Someone stole Phineas's war bonnet."

"Oh, no. Who'd do a thing like that?"

"Try the whole darn fort to start with, Ivy. Though they figure it was a bunch of kids."

"What happened? What did they do with it?"

He grinned and took a long swig of milk.

"Someone shinnied up the flagpole. Tied it right below the flag."

"Is it there still?"

"No, they had to take it down. Someone must have told Phineas about it. He took to doing his dances round the pole, screeching and chanting and carrying on."

"Poor Phineas," I cried, then burst out laughing. I could picture him so vividly. "Sometimes I really miss him, Hamlet, and the fascinating stories he told."

"I know," he said, and paused to watch me, in a musing sort of way. "You miss a lot of things, but you never say it. I never hear you complain anymore, Ivy."

"You don't?" I said, flushed with sudden pleasure.

He pushed back his chair and came to stand beside me.

"I love you," he said. "I just want to tell you that."

He was having trouble finding words—that was rare for Hamlet. But I could look in his eyes and find what I needed there and save him the awkward task of trying to tell me.

"Say that again," I whispered.

"What? I love you?"

"Yes, say it again. That's all I need to hear."

It was late November, and what they called Indian summer—mellow days when the sun still flavored the air, but the breeze had a tangy bite to it. Days of squash and pumpkin and spicy leaves, assailing my senses with beauty and fragrance and peace.

All one morning I had worked in the barn with Hamlet, cleaning the stalls, mending and fixing things. Once or twice I hinted that I had better get back to my kitchen, but he seemed always loathe to let me go. I didn't mind. The new hay, the smell of the leather, the filtering sunbeams playing across the floor filled me with a heady exhilaration, and I'd far rather have been with Hamlet than working alone.

Once he left on an errand for a few minutes, and I sank down in the fresh straw he had spread. I leaned against the boards and closed my eyes, content to only feel and smell and listen.

It was merely a matter of weeks and then, if the miracle happened, I would be a mother! This awkward thing inside that kicked and poked me, that made my back ache and kept me awake at night, would soon become a face, a name—a person! I allowed myself an extravagant luxury—I thought about the baby—as painful, as dangerous as that was. This baby had to be warm and real, and all right!

Hamlet came back and fell right to work once more, but it was way past time to eat and I was starving, so Hamlet finally agreed to stop. He was one to finish a job once he'd begun it.

"I'll help you," he said. "We'll find something to fill you up."

The house seemed cool and dim after the sunlight, but the smells were unmistakable: fresh bread and stewed tomatoes, and something warm with apples in it. The table was set—for three—and someone was standing, hands on hips, surveying me in my confusion, her kind, freckled face beaming delightedly.

"It's about time. I was beginning to wonder if I'd have to eat all this food myself!"

"Jane!" I cried, and flew into her arms. How comforting it was to hug her. She smelled as she always had, like clean rose water. She was childhood and security again. She was sanity, laughter, and hope.

Hamlet stood watching, his own eyes fairly dancing. This was his moment of triumph, his surprise.

"How did you do it, Hamlet?" I demanded, then didn't give him time to answer me.

We cried and laughed and dried each other's tears, and talked more than we ate until finally, Hamlet pushed back his chair in mock disgust.

"I've had enough of female chatter! You two carry on, I've got work to do."

I wouldn't let him go until he kissed me, and I had whispered another thank you into his ear.

"It's hard to believe you're really here," I told Jane. "If I turn around you won't disappear?"

"No chance, dearie. You're stuck with me for awhile."

I laughed. "You've no idea how good that sounds."

The pains were coming regularly—and harder, much harder than before.

"Sit down, you ninny. I've never seen the likes—pacing up and down the way you do."

Poor Jane was red-faced, trying to contain me.

"It helps," I assured her. "Really it does."

"Well, this baby's ready to come, heaven knows. Don't know how you've managed to drag him around with you these past weeks."

It was true. The baby seemed big and very awkward. I was glad there wasn't a proper mirror in the house; it was easier not seeing myself at all. Secretly, I feared what I'd look like afterward. I didn't see how I could ever be "normal" again.

"Now, don't be afraid. I'm sure they'll be here in plenty of time, dearie."

I smiled. "I'm not afraid, Jane."

I truly wasn't. I felt numb and detached, almost as though this was a dream, not happening to the real me at all. It was Jane who was frightened, much as she tried to hide it.

"I told Hamlet," she had said a dozen times, "I'd be glad to come for comfort and company, but he'd better have someone else here for the practical side."

So Hamlet had gone to fetch Lydia for the "practicalities," as Jane called them.

When at last they arrived, I had given up the pacing, and much to Jane's relief, lay obediently on the bed. Lydia was in charge from the moment she entered, and for a good twenty minutes nothing was said while Hamlet and Jane rushed about to fulfill her orders.

"Well," she said, hands on her hips as she looked at Hamlet. "Thank you, young man. I won't be needing you any longer."

She winked at him along with the dismissal. I think Hamlet managed a thin smile, but nothing that remotely resembled his usual. He walked over to where I lay and covered my hand where it rested across the covers.

"Ivy..."

I'd never seen him this way before: awkward, uncertain, in an agony of his own. Never—except for that one other time.

"I'll be all right..."

He bent, smoothed back my hair from across my wet forehead, and kissed me very tenderly.

"Hurry up there, young man. You two are a sight to see!" Lydia bustled him off toward the door.

"Think he'll still moon that way at number thirteen?" Jane's eyes crinkled with lines of laughter as she spoke.

"Him? Most probably. He'll never learn any better."

What fun those two were having. I started to laugh with them, but the tightening began inside, and this time it was deeper and sharper, and longer. I thought it would never peak and dissolve. Jane placed a new, cold cloth across my forehead.

"Relax now, dearie. Try to relax."

I was brave. Later both of them made much of that fact. Lydia did little things to ease me, spent long spells just holding my back in a way that made the pain much easier, but after a certain point nothing helped.

"Leave me alone. This baby won't come," I kept saying.

At last I grew too exhausted to care. And then, when I thought the pain would eat through me, Lydia's face swam into my vision, and I knew by the glow of her eyes that something was happening.

"Push again, love. Push as hard as you can."

I obeyed her, crying out for the first time—and hearing, miraculously, an answering cry. I lifted my head in wonder, and gazed at my son. And this time I cried out with joy.

"Give him to me," I demanded. "Give him to me!"

Jane began to fuss and refuse me, but Lydia remembered the time before. Deftly she wrapped him in a blanket and placed him gently into my arms. He felt small and wet and warm against me. I was anxious to examine every feature, but tears were clouding my eyes. There seemed nothing I could do to stop them. I touched his silken cheek, his little hand, and the tiny fingers curled to meet me. At that moment, the pain came back.

"Lydia!" cried Jane, her voice thick with panic.

When I saw Lydia's face go white, I closed my eyes and prayed. What could be happening to me now?

Then suddenly, Lydia's clear, high laugh made my eyes shoot open.

"Ivy, push again," she cried out. "I don't believe this!"

I did as she told me.

"Harder," she demanded.

Jane gently picked up my newborn son. I didn't object, but clenched my hands into fists and worked with Lydia and the pain. I felt the baby come, I heard the cry, and then laughed out loud in astonishment.

"Well, aren't you the fancy one?" Jane's round eyes were popping with wonder. "S'pose you couldn't decide which kind you wanted, so thought you'd just take one of each."

Lydia handed me the little girl. I must have been both laughing and crying together.

"Is she all right?"

Lydia nodded. "They both seem fine and healthy, hon'."
I touched the curve of her cheek, her thick black hair.
And to think, I mused, *that I murmured at the Lord.*

Finally they admitted Hamlet, but Lydia hadn't really
told him a word.

"Things are just fine, son. You come in and see for
yourself."

Poor Hamlet. Three pairs of eyes were glued to his face.
He walked up slowly, and I watched his eyes grow wide. He
looked from Jane to Lydia, then back to me. Then he
stopped, as though he didn't dare come any closer.

"Get over there, boy. You'll never know what they look
like from this far back."

For the second time that day, Lydia urged him gently.
He came, and the wonder deepened in his eyes.

Jane was bustling right behind his elbow.

"See here," she said, "a daughter for Ivy, and a son for
you!"

But when he bent to pick up one of the babies, it was
the tiny girl he lifted into his arms.

"She's nearly as beautiful as you are, Ivy."

When he brought her back, he knelt beside the bed. I
ran my fingers lightly through his hair. The miracle had
happened and we were one, in a way that was almost too
awesome to understand.

"Remember the words you used when you blessed me?"
I asked him.

"Yes," he replied. "It left me a bit uneasy. I didn't say
you shall bear this child, but you shall bear children. I
wondered why at the time. I hadn't meant to say it that
way."

"I wondered, too," I confided. "I feared perhaps it meant
yet more patience and waiting."

"And all the time," he said softly, "it meant—them."

He touched the little body that rested beside him. His

hand was larger than the tiny face. I reached for his hand and kissed the roughened fingers, then searched his eyes, where I always could read his heart. I had never seen them so filled with love before.

11

Joyful tidings, girl.—
And joy comes well in such a needy time.
SHAKESPEARE

L ydia stayed somewhat longer than she had intended,
and the two of them
spoiled me in every way they knew how. I loved it. It left me
free to care for the babies, to spend all the time I needed
nursing them, cooing over them, discovering their needs,
learning to know them as only a mother can. Of course,
three mothers any day are better than one, and that's
exactly what the two little babies had. Hamlet complained
that there was never one left for him! It was truly a time of
warmth—of suspended happiness and I fed on it, as a
hungry man feeds on meat.

When Lydia did leave at last, I missed her and I knew
that Jane missed her too. But the days were drawing us
nearer to Christmas, and suddenly there were dozens of
things to do—wonderful things that made each day an
adventure and sprinkled a sense of excitement through the
hours.

I hadn't told Jane much about Christmas last year. Even
with two plump babies on my lap, it was difficult to look
back on the blackness and pain. Perhaps Lydia had given her

more of the story. I wasn't sure. Jane's only comment that touched on the situation came one morning when she was gathering up her spices, trying to decide which fruit breads and cakes to bake.

"Now, you mustn't forget the customs of your own people. And I guess if I don't teach you, nobody will. How long has it been since Hamlet tasted plum pudding?"

She glanced up, her bright eyes crinkling at the corners.

"Too long. This year, we shall celebrate Christmas, dearie!"

The names for the babies seemed to come naturally. The boy would be Daniel, after Hamlet's father—first son of his own eldest son; it seemed proper that way. The girl—the girl would be Margaret, after my mother, but with something added—Margaret Deseret. The name to us embodied all our lives stood for, all we had suffered, all the dreams we had planted here.

There was snow for Christmas, deep white drifts of it driven by the wind into marvelous shapes: mounds and peaks, pinnacles and towers, checkerboards of fluff along the fence. Hamlet drove Jane far enough into the mountains to gather fresh, green pine boughs to cover the mantel, with a touch of red, winter berries tucked here and there. We had no mistletoe, no groups of carolers, but we decorated a Yule log and concocted a wassail—using cider in place of the ale— but with roasted apples, eggs, sugar, and all the delicious spices that should be there. And, of course, plum pudding. There were so many things to delight us!

We laughed and talked together about old times, and were entertained by the babies for hours on end. We exchanged little gifts we had made for each other, and basted the turkey, and set out the holiday foods. My heart was filled with thanksgiving the whole day through.

As evening drew near, we sat before the fire and read Luke's account of the Christ child, then turned to the Book of Mormon and what happened here, in this very land, at the time of the Saviour's birth. America—Zion—words that held too much for them to be spoken without something stirring deep in our hearts. We sang the timeless carols of Christmas: "God Rest Ye Merry Gentlemen" and "Joy to the World," "Hark, the Herald Angels Sing," and slowly, lovingly, last of all, "Silent Night."

When Jane was asleep and the babies settled, Hamlet and I took a walk in the still, cold night. The snow crunched beneath our feet, and our breath hung white and frosty on the chill air. There was too much beauty and too much joy to speak. We were aware, with a sudden clearness, of all we were, and, with a deep stirring, a sense of what we might become—together. We were part of something grander, something whole, that could draw us out beyond ourselves— and make us whole and wonderful, too.

"We have doubled since last Christmas," I said.

"It didn't seem possible then," Hamlet murmured, "that we could ever find this much happiness. And yet, it's just beginning isn't it, Ivy?"

I smiled, and shivered, and looked up at the curtain of sky and the hard, brilliant stars that glistened and glittered across it. I felt young and strong and sure of myself again. I wasn't the same person I had been a year ago. I was more than I had been before. I was different inside. I was willing to challenge fate and begin again.

January was mild that year. We steeled ourselves for the storms, but they never came.

Jane promised to stay a few more weeks.

"Those big boys of mine," she declared, "can get on without me. Mayhap they'll appreciate their old mother when I get home."

Jane had four, fine sons, but I had always been her only daughter, spoiled by two mothers as long as I could remember.

Busy in the lean-to kitchen one morning, thinking of

my tired back and the babies to bathe, I was startled to feel a hand grab at my shoulder, and Jane's excited breathing against my ear.

"Ivy, my lands, there's a bunch of redmen out there!"

She was trying to whisper, but her voice kept rising in fear so that each word ended in a shrill note or a little squeak.

"Really?" I asked, turning wide eyes upon her.

"Hoards of them. Heaven save us, where's that Hamlet? Where's the gun?"

"Well, Jane, do you really think they're dangerous?"

"Painted all gruesome, with bows and knives at their belts? And one of em's dancin' around all crazy-like. Makes my skin crawl. Here, child, help me bolt this door."

We had reached the front of the cabin and I was struggling against the smile that wanted to spoil my fun. How far I had come from my own early days of terror! One glance told me that Yanno was the crazy, dancing Indian. I slipped past Jane and darted out to greet him. He saw me and produced his welcoming grin, and with his usual bound leapt up beside me.

I opened my mouth, but never said a word. A teeth-rattling scream rang out behind us, and two hefty, freckled arms, one of them wielding my heavy rolling pin, began beating on Yanno.

I pulled Jane back, feeling guilty to my toes. It was my fault, but I hadn't expected this fierce, motherly protection—nor the hysteria it seemed to unleash.

Poor Yanno. I had never seen *him* at a loss before. He just stood there beneath the blows looking dazed and, it seemed to me, a little frightened.

"You get away from her, you loathsome savage! You hear. Don't you lay a finger on this girl!"

"Jane, it's all right, it's all right!" I kept repeating, pulling back on the arm that held the weapon.

"Friends," I screamed into her ear. "They're friends.

They won't hurt us, Jane. They won't hurt us."

At last she seemed to hear through her own wild rantings. She stopped, poised, looking much like a startled Titan. I snatched the rolling pin from her hand and gently led her off a little way.

"You—know those Indians! Is that what you said?" She looked dazed, as disbelief replaced rage on her honest face.

"Oh, Jane, forgive me. I should have told you at first, but I didn't know it was Yanno. And you were so darling, with your hackles up—"

"Why, you little vixen," she cried. "I ought to turn you over my knee the way I used to!"

I skipped and dodged her friendly blow, but couldn't hold my laugher in any longer.

"Now you're laughing at me!" she cried in indignation. She pushed up her sleeves and tucked in some straying hair. "First you torment me and then you laugh at my suffering. I declare, dearie, this desert sun's addled your wits."

A smile was struggling across her broad features, and I saw the corner of her own mouth twitch.

"You, I'm afraid, are the crazy one," I giggled. "You've convinced *them* of that," I assured her.

She looked where I motioned. The Indians stood in a group, huddled uncertainly, watching the scene before them. She looked from their faces to mine, then the smile broke through. She shook her head back and forth as we laughed together.

"I give up," she sighed. "You win."

Then she pulled off her shawl, spread it out on the winter ground, and sat down right where she was with her arms tucked about her.

"I was always one for adventure," she said with a sparkle. "Folks'll be tickled to hear this when I get home."

I walked toward where Yanno stood, patiently waiting. I hoped I could explain things to him somehow. But I needn't have worried. He smiled when I started talking.

83

"Another crazy, white squaw," he said.

"Yes," I agreed, "another crazy, white squaw."

Then it was our turn to laugh together.

I noticed a young squaw detach herself from the group and drift, it seemed, toward Yanno and me. Then I saw that he was insistently motioning with his hand for her to come forward. She hesitated. I looked at her questioningly, then back at Yanno.

"Your squaw?" I asked.

He couldn't help grinning then, and pushing out his fine chest in a boastful way. But he knit his brow and frowned in her direction, for the poor thing hadn't ventured any closer.

"Oh, Yanno," I cried. "I'm afraid we've frightened her."

I moved quickly, as I spoke, to where she stood, hoping to save her the frightening effort. Yanno pranced beside us, delighted.

"Tash-a, my squaw," he declared with dignity.

Then he nodded toward me.

"I-vy. White woman. Tig-a-boo—friend. Beautiful friend," he solemnly told the girl.

She nodded, her soft eyes searching my own gaze.

I smiled. "Beautiful friend," he had said. I heard Jane mutter something behind me.

I took Tash-a's hand and held it just a moment. It was small and soft and exquisitely formed.

"I am pleased to meet you," I said in my warmest manner.

Yanno beamed on us both.

"She's lovely," I said. "Tash-a is beautiful too."

Her dark eyes warmed. Then she did understand! Yanno nodded, approving of what I had said.

Then I did something I had never done before. I invited Yanno and all of his friends inside! Jane's eyebrows shot up, she jumped to her feet, and hovered around me, though she didn't protest out loud. I was glad, for I felt quite uncomfortable myself.

"Surprise," I said, as I led Yanno to the door. "Surprise," I repeated, wishing I knew his words.

Some of the Indians stayed stubbornly outdoors, Yanno didn't urge them, so neither did I. He and his bride were the first to enter behind me. I seated them, trying to smooth their awkward discomfort. The young squaw's eyes darted eagerly over the room, brimming with curiosity and wonder. Yanno struggled to maintain his superior calm, the swaggering pride so important in his own eyes.

I went quickly to the cradle where the babies lay sleeping, hesitated a moment, then picked up Daniel. He squirmed a little and crinkled up his eyes. I held him out to Yanno.

"Tow-ats-en." I could hear the pride in my voice. "Baby—my new son—Tow-ats-en."

He made a low sound of exclamation and reached for the child. Jane drew in her breath as I placed the little bundle into his lean, brown arms. Tash-a bent over the baby, her dark eyes shining. She made soft, cooing little noises far back in her throat. I couldn't believe how thrilled, how excited I was. Yanno kept shaking his head and chuckling in delight.

"Wait!" I cried, and hurrying back to the cradle, whisked up the wide-eyed, startled Deseret, and laid her in the arms of the Indian girl.

"Tow-ats-en—my daughter," I cried, my voice filled with laughter.

Yanno and his bride were too startled to laugh.

"Good," I said. "Two babies instead of one."

Yanno smiled then and I could see the remembrance in his eyes. He handed the baby back to me solemnly.

"Mormon God remember. Give you two—child. Make you—happy."

It was a long speech, and I wanted to hug him when it was through, but I only answered his solemn nod with my own. Then we feasted together on buttermilk and fresh bread, spread thick with Lydia's sweet, homemade jam. The Indians laughed and grunted and exclaimed to one another. At last I relaxed—and finally, Jane did too.

When they rose to leave, there were many thanks, much hand shaking, and low, friendly murmurs in words I did not understand. Tash-a was the last to leave. She rose slowly.

"Thank you, Tig-a-boo," she said. Her voice held the musical murmur of deep, stream waters.

Carefully she handed me the baby which she had held and caressed and cuddled the whole while.

The best, as well as the worst, must end in its own time.

February came, and with it the date that Brother Olsen from the fort was to drive Jane back to Salt Lake. She left with many a tear and last-minute instructions, with "one last kiss" a dozen times for each baby's cheek. It was very hard to hug her for the last time. For one weak moment I longed to run away with her. She promised again and again that she would return, and she carried a list, a magical list with her, a wish-list of little, city luxuries. She promised to send them, and I knew she would.

As soon as she left, the house seemed silent and empty. Both babies awoke and cried, and I felt sudden panic. There was no one to help. There was no one now but me.

I turned Deseret on her tummy and nursed her brother, hummed to them, and both of them settled down. I sang and rocked and realized, in the quiet, how happy I really was. Jane was wonderful—Jane was a part of me. But so were these little bundles that rested beside me. They had come into my humble house and made it a home. It would never be the same now that they were here.

They held my days in their silken-fine, rosebud hands. In their powerful little grasp they held my life. I belonged to them, and the future they would bring.

12

Witness my son,
Now in the shade of death.

SHAKESPEARE

Two weeks after Jane left, a wagon train passed our way. It was a group of Saints headed for new settlements farther south. They didn't stop long, but while we visited, the children played and ran free. Two or three of the youngsters, ragged and dirty, kept pestering me to let them hold the babies, but they were coughing and their noses were running. As soon as I could, I rescued my little ones and deposited them safely inside the cabin.

Several days later, Daniel began to run a fever. Soon he had trouble breathing, and his throat looked red. A hard knot of fear, like a hand of iron, grabbed me inside. I separated him from Deseret, and bathed his hot, little body with cool cloths. I even knelt at his bedisde and said a prayer. To lose him now would be a hundred times worse than what I had sufferd before.

When Hamlet came in he found me walking the floor with his son. Fear, like a flame, leapt into his clear, blue gaze. He came to me and took the child into his own strong arms.

"Dyptheria," I whispered. I had seen it too many times.

"Deseret?"

"She seems all right, so far," I answered.

We spoke in new voices, low and subdued, carefully unemotional. We did not name the intruder who had laid his hand upon us, nor talk outright of the dread of him both of us shared. We must battle this enemy now on the terms he dictated, and both of us knew the cost if death won the victory.

I urged Hamlet to eat the simple meal I'd prepared for him. I think he tried, but the food stuck in his throat, he said.

We took turns watching and sitting with Daniel through the night, clearing the mucus from his throat, cooling his hot skin. We said little. What comfort could words bring, what release from our torturing thoughts?

About midnight, Hamlet ran a hand through his disheveled hair, dragged his boots toward him, and began to pull one on.

"I'm going to find a doctor."

He didn't look up as he spoke.

A thrill—half relief, half hopelessness—spread over me.

"Hamlet—"

"Don't Ivy. It's useless to discuss it. I've made up my mind."

"You're dead tired. You can't just leave in the middle of the night this way."

He rose and lifted his jacket from the peg where it hung. I noticed how worn the elbows were, how frayed the edges.

"Hamlet!" There was more censure in my voice than I had intended. "What if—what if something should—happen—while I'm alone with him?"

"Ivy, my darling, it can't. It won't."

There were dark circles under Hamlet's eyes, and his skin was ashen.

"Come here," he said, and pulled me against him tenderly. "He won't die, Ivy. You've got to believe he's not going to die."

I tasted the sharpness of salt on my tongue, and realized I was crying. How long? I wondered. Hamlet's eyes were winter blue and clear. He drew me down beside him and we knelt together and pleaded for the life of our son. Then Hamlet turned and left me alone in a prison of pain and dread.

Happiness can eat up the hours with hungry ease, but pain draws out the minutes like hard kernels of sand through a protesting needle's eye. There was no clock in the house to tidily proportion the agony. I could only guess at how long it took to pace the room, stand over the little body, then turn and pace again. Back and forth, back and forth, a dozen times—twenty—thirty. I counted the footsteps, then lost track, and started all over again.

At one point, I became vaguely aware that the sky was lightening with streaks of grey that spread and widened, but there was no sun. A gloomy daylight marked the coming day, and within the little cabin there was no change.

Deseret awoke, but she didn't cry. I picked her up and checked her nose and throat. Her color was good. She felt cool after handling Daniel. I bathed and dressed her, then sat in the rocker to let her nurse, yet close enough to watch Daniel's listless form. I tried to sing, but the music unleashed my tears. That, of course, would never do. I walked to the window for perhaps the hundredth time and searched for a shape in the distance that might mean Hamlet. Nothing. No sign of any living thing appeared.

What am I doing here? something within me cried *in the middle of nowhere, watching my little boy die?*

It was noon. I could tell it was noon, by the place of the sun, high and pale in the gloom of the winter sky. I picked up my son and held him against my heart. I talked to him as though he could understand. I told him about the day my father died; how my mother sat at her window and wouldn't cry; how his boots stood beside the brazier where he had left them, and the pipe he had lit filled the room with its sweet aroma; and I kept watching to see him lean over the arm of his chair and ask me to sit at his knee as I always had done.

I told him how it was when I left England; how I polished the wood in my room very carefully and straightened the drawers and the bookshelves and smoothed the bed; how I pulled the first yellow rose from the vine by my window and carried it until it wilted and fell apart.

I told him of the night my mother died; how she called for me and told me what she could see; how she spoke to my father as though he were there beside her; how she thought she saw the valley before she died, and she never knew that we buried her in Wyoming, in a shallow grave, with no coffin at all—never knew how I held the lantern to light him while Brother Edwards carved her name on a crude, wooden marker.

I told him of how it was when we entered the valley; what it felt like to take those last few steps and stop, knowing we were wanderers no longer. I told him how his father had looked when I saw him—lean and a little cocky, his hair like spun gold, his eyes pools of wonder, his kiss like the first taste of spring.

I told him about the day when we were married, of the sacred feeling that words can't even describe; how I sensed my parents were there, though I couldn't see them. I told him about the joy and celebration, and what it felt like to lie in his father's arms.

I talked on and on and the sound of my voice seemed to soothe him, and he didn't mind the tears when they fell on his cheek. I told him what it was like to lose a baby, and then to hold your first-born son in your arms.

"You must be very careful not to die," I told him. "Too much of me would die with you, you see. And what would be left for Hamlet and your sister?"

The change came about mid-afternoon. He couldn't breathe, his fine skin was turning purple. I had once seen a doctor slit the throat of a child and open the little, choked windpipe so he could draw breath, having only fishhooks to hold back the torn flesh, but I watched my son struggle with a terrible helplessness.

Finally, I knelt with him in my arms. There was always prayer. If life took everything else, it still left that. There on the woven rug we prayed together, and Deseret watched us with wide and wonderful eyes.

That is how Hamlet found us when he walked in. His eyes, terrible, gave me my answer before he could form it into words.

"No doctor," he said, his voice as worn as his face. "Lydia left for Grove Creek yesterday. Four children have died there already."

He stood before me streaked with dirt, exhausted. He had ridden all night and all day; he had tried, and failed. He opened his arms in a helpless, pathetic gesture.

"I've come home to you empty-handed, Ivy," he said. Tears ran down the lines of hopelessness carved on his face.

I rose carefully, supporting the motionless body I carried. I didn't know if Daniel still breathed. I refused to let myself look upon his face.

"This child isn't meant to die," I said.

The words rang warm and true in the silent room. Hamlet brushed back his hair and stared at me. A tiny spark appeared in his drained, blue eyes. There wasn't time to tell him how I knew. We pray, and answers come, but how can we tell it?

"You aren't empty-handed Hamlet," I said. I drew out his arms and laid his son across them, loving him with a pain that was total and sweet.

"Give him a Priesthood blessing, Hamlet. You did all you could to secure the help of men. Remember what Brother Brigham says? You have a right now to ask the

Lord for help."

"Yes." He looked at his hands, he flexed one slowly. "Yes, I have the power," he said.

A thrill shivered through me and ended in pools of gladness, as though a burden was lifting from my heart, lifting from out of my fiber and sinews.

Hamlet placed his hands on the little head, anointed his child, and gave him a father's blessing. Some day there may be a way to record our words—the inflections of the voice, the feeling, the expession. Even words written on paper remain, and live, but each word Hamlet spoke is recorded and sealed in my heart and will burn there much longer than body and flesh survive.

He spoke the word, "amen," and I pulled back the blanket. Daniel's eyes were closed; he was breathing easily. The purple hue no longer tainted his flesh. I placed my hand against the little chest and felt the gentle rhythm of his breath.

I laid the baby down gently in his bed, then turned and opened my arms, and Hamlet came. And I knew what it was to give all I had to give—to welcome the pain and the giving; then to rise—to nearly perish with joy.

They say troubles always come in batches—never by the ounce, but by the pound. So it was with us. We barely had time to catch our breaths and relax into Daniel's recovery when disaster struck in another quarter.

Hamlet went out early one morning to find three of his cattle fevered and lame. It could have been one of half a dozen things, but how to discover and isolate the cause? Then how to treat it? How to save their lives?

As the signs progressed and the animals suffered convulsions, Hamlet recognized the dreaded Blackleg, but the disease had progressed too far for him to check it. Within twenty-four hours, all three of the cows were dead. These were part of his young, new stock—his yearlings. He couldn't afford that kind of loss, and he blamed himself bitterly for his youth and lack of experience. He was convinced that most other men could have prevented the deaths.

It was late March and time for planting, yet there was no rain. We had experienced a mild, dry winter with scant moisture to swell the mountain streams. Hamlet plowed the ground, and waited. Without water there would be no crops. Without crops, no food—no survival. It was that close, that basic, with so little margin for human error, or for the cruel, manipulative tricks that nature played.

A dozen times I picked up my laughing baby, felt him warm and alive in my arms.

"None of it matters," I would whisper against his ear. "It doesn't make any difference. You're here. You live. Nothing can really hurt us now."

Nevertheless, I knew that wasn't entirely true. Life is made up of hard practicalities. Without them, life would cease to exist, cease to progress. We needed to face them, harsh and unyielding as they might be.

There was more. This kind of failure touched on the nerve of Hamlet's pride, down to the core where his manhood lived and took stock of itself. If he failed to provide, if his family suffered because of him, how could he face his tomorrow with self-respect? He had used his power to save his son's life. Now, as he saw it, he had to give something to make that life worthwhile.

As the days stretched on, hot and cloudless, the tension stretched tighter. Hamlet grew silent and moody. I hated to see him that way. I felt stifled, worn out—but pressed down more than anything else by monotony. We didn't laugh, we didn't play—we didn't even seem happy anymore.

I began to grow restless with a thwarted, impatient feeling. I dragged at my work, my mind felt sluggish, my temper was short. When I looked in the Wesley mirror, my face appeared dry and cracked and dull. There were none of the warm, glowing features of an eighteen-year-old girl.

I often had trouble falling asleep at night. My mind became a torture chamber of fears and doubts. Every evil thing that could possibly happen seemed to come to life and find lodging there, plucking away at the raveled edges of my security.

One such night I lay motionless, willing myself to sleep, sensing that Hamlet, beside me, lay wakeful and sleepless too. I felt I would scream if something didn't happen. The thought of tossing and turning and falling asleep at last, then rising to another dismal, dust-filled, discouraging day, filled me with loathing. Restlessness pounded through my veins. It was a lovely night. If only—if only—

"Hamlet." I touched his arm as I spoke. "There's a moon tonight."

He turned easily, as much awake as I.

"So there is." His voice sounded somewhat perplexed, but not sleepy.

He raised himself on his elbow and cocked his head.

"There was a moon last night, you know. And there ought to be one tomorrow night as well."

A little shiver, a thrill went through me. It was his voice—something of the old, careless lilt he had lost for awhile. I sat up, disturbing the bed covers, and hugged my knees. My hair tumbled over my shoulders and swished against my back. Even sitting there I could feel what it would be like for the night wind to lift my hair.

"I can't sleep."

"And what does that have to do with the moon?"

"Everything," I cried. "The moon and the stars and the wide-open fields and the wind in my hair."

He looked at me in a way that sent the blood pulsing through my veins. It never took Hamlet long to catch on to the spirit of things. I knew the lights were leaping into his blue eyes.

"Will the babies sleep?"

"Yes. They'll be fine." I said it softly, holding my breath.

He lifted my hair and let it sift through his fingers like sand.

"My little gypsy, is your wild streak bothering you again?"

His voice, in the intimate darkness, fell on me like a caress. I moved my head so his fingers ran along my cheek, and brushed the fingers gently with my lips. He turned my face and spoke with his mouth against my hair.

"Who am I to deny the moon and the gypsy wind?"

Once out in the night, a sense of excitement ran over me. Night was a different world that had always been barred—held at arm's length by a learned set of fears and by years of unquestioned, blind propriety. But tonight, there was something that whispered and beckoned, inviting me in. There were no shadows, no secrets. Hamlet's warm arm curved around my waist. The sudden staccato clacking of a screech owl, the soft night sounds, carried no fears, but a lingering note of conspiracy. Teah felt it. He pranced as he walked, and threw back his fine head. As I hugged him with my knees I could feel his expectancy run through his flesh and into my own.

So we rode together, we three, as we had never ridden before. The thud of hoofs on the hard earth beat a rhythm, faster and faster, until I could hear them no more, and we were flying, one with the wind and the fragrant air. Gently the night, soft and soothing, stripped back our cares, layer following layer, until our hearts lay bare and our spirits were free to remember, to soar, to dare.

The fields were ours, the ground we covered, the creek, the trees. Why not the stars? Why not the moon in our spot of sky? I tasted life on my skin, on my lips. I drank it in. The whole wide expanse of heaven stretched over me. Was it large enough to hold my dreams?

13

Fear comes upon me;
O, much I fear some ill, unlucky thing.

SHAKESPEARE

The night ride made a difference. It pulled us together again. It kept the music in Hamlet's voice, the brightness in his eyes. I hummed at my work, and we knew what it was to be happy again.

Even so, that was where the magic ended. It couldn't change the skies, mass the air into clouds, and gather them over our heads. We planted and carried water to the seedlings, breaking our backs—breaking our hearts as well. Still no rain. The sliver of water in the creek bed vanished. We were back to mud and mosquitoes again.

One evening, late, when the children were quiet and sleeping, Hamlet drew out his ledgers, his long, narrow record books. He opened them up and busied himself quietly, scribbling and writing and figuring awhile.

"Come over here, Ivy. I want you to see this," he said.

I put down my sewing and pulled up a chair beside his. He showed me the columns: the assets, the losses, the costs, the profits, all tidily arranged. It helped to see it laid out like that—because then I knew. His fears were well-founded. If we lost just one more animal—if this crop failed—then the tidy, black column of figures entitled "losses" would eat up the page and spell nothing but one word—failure—at the end.

"Isn't there anything—"

"No." His voice cut through my question "There'd be no way to feed us or the animals. No way to buy the seed and the tools we need. The next few weeks decide it. It's out of our hands."

He pulled out a paper—a letter—and began to unfold the pages. I recognized Jane's writing.

"Whatever are you doing with that?"

He looked up and turned his steady, blue gaze upon me—so honest, so searching, so dear.

"It's Jane's last letter. I've kept it on purpose, to read now and then just in case I tend to forget."

Whatever could he be talking about? I picked up the letter and scanned it hurridly. I could see nothing special or unusual there.

"But why?" I asked. "What is it that she said?"

"Everything," he replied, in a voice that sent ice through my veins. "The parties, the dinners, the ladies meetings, the sewing bees, the shops, the fine dresses, meetings in the bowery."

His voice bore ruthlessly on like the dry, rustling knell of defeat, "clean streets and water, neighbors and schools—"

"Hamlet, stop!"

He paused, and I filled up the space before he could start again.

"I know all that," I cried. "I've always known it."

"Well then, perhaps you forget that I know it too," he said.

"What do you mean by that?"

He had never talked this way before. It frightened me.

"Don't you think I know what a different world that is?

You'd fit so perfectly into that kind of life, Ivy. Security—maybe even a luxury here and there."

There was a bitterness in his tone that took my breath away: "Schools for the children—doctors." He looked up, his eyes dark.

"Daniel wouldn't have nearly died if we lived in Salt Lake."

"Well, he didn't die here!"

"You know what I mean!" He pushed back his hair. His eyes looked wild in a strange, tired way.

"What about the next time," he cried, "and the next—and the next—"

"Well, what about land of our own?" I threw back at him. "Something we build with our own hands? Something our children can love?"

"What about it?" The words were dead, devoid of feeling or hope.

He pushed back his chair, refolded the letter, and closed his books. I wanted to argue, but something within me drew back, afraid. So we left the question unanswered, hanging silently above our heads.

The day came, as we knew it would, when the water ran out. Hamlet made preparations to go up to the mountains for water again, but that wasn't a solution, it was only holding off. If the rains didn't come . . . but there was no use thinking of that.

There was always a forced naturalness between us at such times, a deliberate holding back from what was happening inside both of us. He kissed me, and in an instant the thought came unbidden to my mind: *What if this is the last time he ever kisses me?* I shuddered and pulled him close and touched his lips again, smoothed out his hair, memorized the lines of his face. It could happen—I had no special, gold-engraved guarantees.

"Take care," I said, hoping he couldn't read my eyes.

He nodded, and I drew back at the despair I read in his own. He had climbed up and started the cumbersome wagon, but I couldn't stop myself.

"Hamlet!"

He cocked his head and looked back.

"I love you," I said.

He stopped and turned in his seat.

"Why did you say that?"

"Because I mean it. Because 'take care' isn't enough."

There was a pause. I could see the play of shadows across his face. At last he smiled, but the smile had only sadness in it. He reached for my hand, and I gave it to him, dismayed.

"Ivy, me and this place—we're millstones around your neck."

He looked at my hand as he spoke, and not at my eyes.

"Stop it, Hamlet! I won't allow you to talk that way."

A cold fear like a sudden gust swept over me.

He smoothed my hand with his, then let it go. The sad smile came again.

"One day I mean to justify your loving me."

He was gone. I stood, as though rooted, and watched him go. When at last I turned and stumbled indoors, it was not with the resolute determination of times before. I sank down on the little, rag rug and cried and cried.

Two hungry voices, shrill and insistent, roused me at last and I stirred myself to the tasks that needed doing. By mid-morning, if not happy, at least I was in control. I could ignore the hollow ache I carried inside.

My salvation lay in the fact that there was so much to do, especially now after wasting my early hours. I settled the babies safely on a quilt on the floor, gave them the rattles and toy blocks Hamlet had made them. Deseret stared at me, sweet and content, with my mother's eyes. Daniel cooed and giggled. His cornflower eyes were his father's, laced with sparkle, never holding still.

I hurried to the barn to finish the chores there. When alone with the children, I always worked in shifts, never leaving them very long at any time. It meant much extra running back and forth for me, but I didn't mind it. It was worth it to know they were well and safe.

The morning, though nearing noon, was cool still and smelled of spring. Vague, tantalizing fragrances teased at my memory, whispy reminders of the full promise yet to come. Tranquil, and yet refreshing, the air trickled over me, sending wonderful sensations along my skin.

I sighed. I breathed deeply. The brown fields were bathed in dew, the trees cast showers of pearls on me as I passed. A fierce, possessive pride stirred in me. Things would work out. They had to. This was home—not just a plot hemmed in by other plots, an impersonal niche in a city that didn't care. This was land a man could walk over for more than half the day without reaching the end of what he called his own: hillocks and pastures, willows, wild berries, and streams. This was the freedom of silence and sunshine and wind. This was the purity of new love planted deep.

I carried two heavy buckets of milk as I walked into the cabin, so I didn't see the figure sitting across from me. Awareness swept over me when I heard the harsh scrape of boots on the wood, a rasping laugh that was more like a growl. My heart seemed to burst and send stinging arrows all through me, then shrink and contract and sit like a hard stone against my breast.

A voice came out of the shadows. "So this is the little lady of the house," it said. The voice held a rasp, like the laugh, but the words were sloppy and slurred.

Slowly I raised my eyes and looked at the man.

He was thirty-five, perhaps even forty. He wore no beard, but an unshaven stubble of purple shadowed his chin. His eyes were large and set far back in his head. His hair was greasy, his clothes black with grease and dirt. I could smell the stench of old sweat and fresh liquor even from where I stood. I tried to force my mind to think. My legs felt weak and watery, my hands, where I clenched them at my sides, were warm and damp.

"What are you doing here in my house?" I had spoken the necessary words, but they sounded weak, with no note of authority in them.

Unconsciously I cast my eyes to the wall. The loaded Hawken was gone from its place.

"Right here," he said and patted his knee.

I saw that my rifle lay across his lap.

"I thank ye kindly for loadin' it for me, ma'am," Then he grabbed his pocket and shook it against his leg. "Got any more of these I didn't find?"

"Guns and bullets? Is that what you want?" I said.

"That's a good beginning."

I took a step, and his eyes became instantly cautious and dark.

"Look, honey, I'm here, and I ain't in no hurry to leave. So the sooner you get used to that fact, the better."

I was shaking all over. I felt my whole body go weak.

"My husband—" I began, but his harsh laugh stopped me.

"Your husband, sweetie, just drove out of here this morning. That gives us two—mebbe three days alone together."

His eyes traveled over me slowly, and I shrank back.

"How did you know?" I couldn't help asking the question.

"That's my secret, little gal. You jest remember there ain't much around here old Ethan doesn't know."

He threw back his head and took a swig from a bottle, noisily, with a relish that made me sick.

"Stop starin' at me like some kinda skeert wild rabbit. I ain't gonna hurt you. Why don't you take care a this kid?

He's makin' me nervous, hollerin' like a stuck pig."

I hadn't even realized Daniel was crying. I bent and swept him up into my arms. I could feel the man's eyes follow my every motion. I changed Daniel, cooed and whispered and tried to soothe him, but he could feel the tension in my arms. I knew very well what his problem was, he was hungry. But how could I feed him under those watchful eyes?

"The brat wants his dinner."

I hesitated—I froze. Every muscle in my body was rigid with fear and loathing, and a sickness was working its way up into my throat.

The man wiped a dribble from his mouth with the back of his hand.

"Hell, feed 'im. You think I aint never seen a woman before?"

The words were casual, even indifferent, but the leer that spread over his face was not.

I walked carefully over and sat on the edge of the bed, expecting my fragile control to break any moment. With my back to the man I carefully undid my dress and held my breath as Daniel began to suck, tensed for the slightest movement, the slightest sound.

The man continued drinking and left me alone.

That was the worst of the day. Somehow, after that, I was able to function, keep from being choked by the fear, overcome by the treacherous weakness that threatened to sap my strength.

I cooked a meal for Ethan, but I couldn't eat. He ate voraciously, but he drank even more. By late afternoon, his speech had grown very garbled. He sat back in my rocker, his glassy eyes half-closed.

Forbidden to leave the house, I was trapped with him. Earlier I had foolishly tried to persuade him.

"It will look suspicious if the animals aren't tended to."

"Suspicious?" he snorted. "To who? The skunk rats and coyotes?"

Of course he would know. There were no other homesteads, no people, no life within miles of here. I refused to let myself think about tomorrow—what might happen to me alone for days with this man. Even the beginnings of the thought nearly drove me crazy, paralyzing me with an aching fear.

I resolved to live one day at a time, one hour, one creeping minute: clear up the dishes, rock Deseret to sleep, mend Hamlet's shirt, wash the smoky, lamp chimneys—anything to keep my fingers busy, to help drive the thoughts away.

But I wondered, through the hours, what brought him here. Finally I determined to find out.

"Who's after you?" I asked. "What have you done?"

"Hell, nothin'."

I had caught him off guard.

"A man can't even spit in peace nowadays."

I didn't reply. With some show of muttering and groaning he went on.

"So I sprung a few traps. They was workin' my territory. A man's got a right."

He glanced up and I faintly nodded.

"That and the grub and the money—that was all. Teach 'em a lesson. But now I gotta lay low for awhile."

I wanted to ask, "And then?" But I bit my tongue.

The last of the daylight flitted slowly away, and the last of the whiskey trickled over his tongue.

I fed the babies and laid them down to sleep, then invented things to do as the night wore on. I knew some kind of confrontation must come, but what would it be, and how was I to face it?

Ethan, like some cruel, bearded spectre, snored in the chair, but my rifle was locked securely over his knees. Perhaps when he slept soundly—perhaps what? If only

Teah were here I could ride like the wind, cover miles in minutes—and leave my babies with him? I shuddered. Could I try walking through the ink black night, one child on each arm, all the way to the fort? There were no possibilities, nothing to do. I was at his mercy, and he knew it as well as I.

I was tired, but I forced myself to move, until after what seemed like a long time, he hadn't stirred. Cautiously, I stretched out across the bed, on top of the spread quilt, all of my clothes still on. I tried to rest, but I fought against actually closing my eyes. If I did, I would be defenseless . . . until perhaps it would be too late . . .

With a sudden snort, Ethan roused and rose up in his chair. The rockers creaked. I could hear his hand fumbling, reaching for a bottle, then a livid curse when he realized that not one of them held a drop.

"There's room in that bed for both of us, don't you think?"

He rose clumsily and stumbled toward me.

I sat up quickly.

He laughed, deep down in his throat, and the sound sent cold chills in wave after wave washing over my flesh.

"A cold bed's no comfort. I'll keep you warm, my pretty."

The ugly laugh came again. I slipped smoothly away as he moved and sat heavily down on the bed beside me. But I was no longer there. He cursed again. His eyes were bloodshot circles, angry and dark. He rose and lunged for me, but I stepped aside.

"Don't play your games with me," he snarled.

I could read cold determination in his eyes, but the drink inside him played havoc with his control. I closed my eyes and prayed silently. Then, as if on cue, Daniel started to cry.

"Shut that kid up!"

I moved even as he spoke. I picked Daniel out of the

crib, but I held him in an uncomfortable position. When he stuck first his fist, then his fat thumb into his mouth, I ruthlessly pulled it out again. Daniel kept crying. Ethan swayed as he watched, and his eyes grew dull.

"Hell," he muttered. "I ain't good for nothin' but sleep."

He clicked open the rifle and emptied it into his lap, adding the bullets to those he carried in his pants pocket.

"There, that oughtta fix ya." He sprawled out across the bed. "But jest in case it don't, hand me that kid."

I froze as if struck.

"Come on now," he demanded.

"Not him," he said, as I fumbled with Daniel's wraps. "The quiet one. That's a good girl. Lay 'er down right here."

I lifted Deseret in my arms. She stirred and smiled faintly. I smoothed her cheeks and prayed with all my soul. Then I laid her against the stranger's arm, and he drew her close with a short, hard laugh—close enough for her to feel his soured breath on her face, close enough that I could never snatch her away. And the rifle, unloaded, rested under his other hand.

Somehow—much later—I prayed myself to sleep, wishing that just once, tomorrow would never come.

14

*But this all lies
within the will of God,
To whom I do appeal.*

SHAKESPEARE

When morning intruded, it took me a long, long time to fight off the solace of sleep, as though my brain retained the reluctance I'd impressed on it the day before. The horror of my situation sunk in by degrees, but there was no way I could ignore it, no place to run and hide.

I moved reluctantly out of the warm circle of drowsiness, hugging the false security as long as I could. Then my eyes flew open suddenly, bringing me wide awake. Deseret! How could I have forgotten that my baby was with that man!

I turned my eyes, and my heart caught suddenly in my throat. The bed was mussed and rumpled—and empty. I ran to the corner. Deseret slept peacefully in her cradle. Daniel lay blinking up at me with wide, blue eyes. I smiled, and sparkles leapt into his watching eyes. I felt my breath return and my heart relax.

"You greedy little thing," I teased. "You're always the first one up and the first one fed. All you leave is leftovers for your sister."

My voice sounded bright, almost happy with relief.

"Well, today my breakfast comes first. His'll have to wait."

The harsh voice startled my peace with a sickening jar. For one, warm, fleeting moment had I really forgotten the man?

He pushed through the door, not closing it behind him, and threw a side of bacon across the table. The morning light seemed to burst through the little room, too bright, too stark. I winced. He felt it too. His eyes were slits, he held his head and moaned.

"Get movin', woman. I need some food in me."

So it went. He peppered my hours with harsh demands. He couldn't find any more whiskey, and he didn't like that. I realized then that the drink had been my friend. It had mellowed him, disarmed him, calmed him down. Without the whiskey, he was little and mean.

And tonight—without the whiskey? But that wouldn't do. If I thought about tonight I would scream—I would die. I must think only about my babies, not myself.

Sober, Ethan wasn't so relaxed. His tension drew him taut as a tightened string.

"Damn. When will that man of yours be back? Today— mebbe tomorrow—I gotta get gone!"

He stressed the last word and rubbed his stubbled chin.

"I need that horse a' his if I'm gonna get very far."

It struck me then so that suddenly I felt quite weak, and a dizziness started humming in my head. He meant to take Hamlet's pony when he returned. Teah! A sudden memory of our last ride together flashed and was gone.

Surely after Ethan took a man's food and money and horse—surely he didn't leave the man to just stand there and watch?

As the day wore on, I began to feel sick with dread and the constant pressure of moving and working beneath his eyes. I fed him a noon meal and that relaxed him a little. He propped the now loaded rifle against the wall, leaned back in his chair, and closed his sunken eyes.

I heard the shuffled footsteps instantly, but forced myself not to turn and alert Ethan. Whoever was out there became now, through force of circumstance, my ally. I choked down the hope that rose in me unbidden.

The door was ajar.

I heard the soft footsteps draw closer. A slight, brown arm pushed the door with a little creak. Then a soft voice spoke at my elbow.

"Bread? Any bread?"

Ethan had jumped to his feet, wide awake now. He reached for the rifle and cradled it in his arms.

The Indian woman clutched at her dirty sack. Her hair was lank and dirty, her thin shawl grey.

"Bread? Any bread?" she repeated, without looking up. But her voice had the sound of water rippling through it . . . a sound I surely remembered.

"What's goin' on? Get that filthy squaw out of here!"

"She's harmless. It won't hurt to give her a little bread."

I was surprised at how strong and controlled my voice sounded.

"She'll go away faster that way," I added.

Ethan hesitated.

"Well, make it snappy."

The squaw raised her eyes, doe-soft in a small, oval face. Fine, high cheekbones, skin like a dusky peach, and a voice like singing waters—Tasha! As I gazed at the lovely features, Ethan examined them too.

"Ummmm, what 'ave we got ourselves? A pretty one here?"

He moved. Tasha drew back, but Ethan kept coming. His face was growing mean and determined now. He brandished the rifle in one hand as he advanced.

"Don't play stupid, honey. You know what I want."

A grin spread over his face and pulled at his mouth. "I'm gonna teach you what happens to squaws that refuse a white man."

He was close to her now.

He reached out to pull her toward him. I saw the mocassined foot move out and strike, tripping the man as he began to lunge.

Ethan fell heavily. The rifle flew out of his hand. I ran and snatched it.

But Ethan was struggling to his feet!

Tasha slipped into a corner. I lowered the gun. Then a shadow bounded lightly through the door, a shadow of substance that struck at the half-crouched man.

Easily, gracefully, the shadow's arm drew back to strike again. It hit with the force of tempered steel, and Ethan's jaw seemed to crumble. He cursed, then groaned as Yanno's foot struck, sinking into Ethan's middle. Deftly the Indian turned him onto his face and bound his arms with a long strip of leather.

Only a matter of seconds and it was over. I stood there trembling, trying to take it all in. I was safe. I was free. I looked into Yanno's anxious, brown eyes where pride struggled with concern for mastery! This Indian—this friend—had saved my life.

Tasha came softly out of the shadows. I drew her toward me and hugged her as I would Jane. She felt light and frail as a bird against me. Her warm eyes glowed, though she dropped them before my gaze.

"Yanno! How can I ever, ever thank you?"

He grinned. "You thank me plenty," he said.

"But how did you know I was in trouble? Did you know Ethan was here?"

Yanno threw out his chest and spoke with relish. He had a spellbound audience with happy, admiring eyes.

"I come. I see no Ivy—no husband in fields. I look around—no cattle fed—no pony—strange horse tied up in barn."

I listened, marveling.

"What I do—without you come to hurt?" He knit his brow. "Then my Tash-a—she give me idea. Yanno know now. My Tash-a—she not afraid. I send Tash-a—I wait—I come. Easy—you see?"

"I see! I see! You're wonderful," I cried.

"Will you stay?" I asked, but Yanno shook his head.

"See babies—then go. This Ethan—wanted man. Yanno take him to his people—get reward money."

"Why is he wanted?" I asked, wanting to know if there was more than Ethan had told me, yet recoiling with a chill at the prospect of an answer.

"He plenty Katz-at—bad, plenty bad. Steal horses— guns. Kill soldier—kill white trader."

I nodded, feeling weak and drained inside. I was grateful that I hadn't known before.

Tasha had drifted over by the babies. "Nan-a pe-ap," she murmured, touching them gently.

I looked at Yanno.

"Your babies grow big—nice," he said and pointed at Tasha with obvious pride.

"See my squaw? Have baby too."

He touched the slight, rounded swell beneath her dress.

Tasha smiled at me with pleasure in her eyes.

"A baby of your own?"

"Oo-ah," she answered, nodding.

"I am happy," I said, taking both of her hands. "Tig-a-boo, thank you. Thank you for being my friends."

Yanno nodded. It would not do to lose his composure.

"Own-shump," he said—it is enough.

He loaded Ethan back onto his worn-out horse. I stayed in the house with Tasha until he was through, and made her promise to bring the baby to see me.

They left, and all the tension dissolved. I realized how exhausted I was. The afternoon was growing warm. I looked around me, discouraged at what I saw—the debris of the past two days still scattered about. I needed to sweep the debris from my mind as well, scrub away the smudges, be clean again.

What to do first? I sunk to my knees by the babies. They wouldn't remember, they wouldn't bear any scars. They were young and pure and strong, able to meet the tomorrows their lives would bring. I too was strong and young, and clean.

I didn't hear the horses or the wagon. My tired mind didn't register a thing until his footsteps crossed the threshold. I turned. He opened up his arms to me. Never had I needed them more! I stayed there, feeling the beating of his heart, close against him, part of him again—whole, as I never could be when we were apart.

How could I begin to tell him of what had happened?

"I know," he said, as if he could read my thoughts. "I know what you've been through. I met Yanno and Tasha. I talked with them. I saw the man."

I had never heard Hamlet's voice sound hard before. Hard and old—and very, very angry.

"It will take awhile for me to settle things here, but I'll arrange for you and the babies to go right away."

I looked up at him, blinking. I couldn't grasp what he was saying.

"Go? Go where?"

"Back to Salt Lake," he said.

"No!" I turned on him fiercely. "Does that mean you're giving up?"

"Ivy, you're overwrought." His voice was tender. "You don't understand—"

"Understand? You're right, I don't. I don't understand how you can turn your back on our dream."

"It was a foolish, boyish dream. I had no right—"

"It's my dream, too," I cried.

"Ivy, what can I do? I promised to care for you, and look

what happens." His voice was filled with tears. "What choice do I have?"

I drew back from him, trembling.

"That's right," I exclaimed. "You have no choice. I refuse to leave."

He looked worried, almost frightened. I took a breath. I had to speak reasonably, calmly, in order to make him see. "*This* is home, Hamlet." I stressed the word lovingly. "We've built every bit of it with our bare hands. We've sanctified it with our pain and joy. I've had my babies here— it's here I've learned to love. I've learned what it is to grow, to be one with a man. I've found myself here, Hamlet. It's part of me."

He was silent, and so we heard the far-off roll, the rumbling that seemed to come from the earth itself. We looked at each other, not hoping, yet holding our breaths. Again, it came, longer and closer than before.

He grasped my hand and we raced outside together. There were clouds above us churning up the sky. A faint, cool breeze blew the taste of rain into our nostrils. The thunder spoke again and a white streak of lightning cut a flaming zigzag across the blue-grey clouds.

"You see," I cried, "the dream wasn't meant to die!"

Hamlet's eyes were on fire. He couldn't answer. Something within me sang at the joy in his eyes. I felt love for him, like a power, surging through me. I thought with a sudden clearness of understanding: *Love isn't something that happens, it's something that grows. And the more it grows, the more it becomes a power, and the more it reveals ourselves to our own eyes.*

"Look, Ivy."

He pulled me close and we looked together. Across the warm, dry fields the curtain of rain was coming. Lines of black that ended in soft, grey mist. The mountains, in the grey-green light of the storm, looked enchanted, unworldly— bathed in a glow that seemed to radiate from within. I could see in bold outline the shape of each tree, each boulder. The mountains were lean and black and alive. I longed to reach out and touch them, to feel the scarred rock surge and tremble beneath my hand.

The rain began to whisper closer now. Then it fell like soft, brushed velvet against our skin.

"The rain is feeding our thirsty dream," I said.

"You are the dream," he answered. "Rain and sun. Cattle and ripened fields. Planting and harvest. Without you, they all would be nothing."

Someone up there knows about my tomorrows. The treasures, the trials—the dreams, the realities. It is enough for me to know what I see before me, to trust the whole to wiser hands than mine. To love, to go on, to weep my portion of tears—to sing my joy.

Home wasn't the wooded countryside of England, lost now in the misty reaches of memory, nor the city of the Saints, new and sparkling, set like a jewel against the desert sands. Home wasn't even the cozy cabin behind me, nor the fields that were turning to mud beneath our feet.

Home was the little circle of Hamlet's arms. I knew this as I had never known it before. I was home in his arms. Nothing else could ever matter.

Epilogue

All yet seems well;
and if it end so meet, The bitter past,
more welcome is the sweet.

SHAKESPEARE

Twenty springs and summers have passed and faded, twenty golden harvests have been gathered in. Twenty times the hand of winter has closed its ruthless hold upon the land, freezing all warmth and life for a season. But the land has survived the winters, and so have we. Survived and come back to fight the floods, the droughts, the dust, the insects—come back to bloom and build again.

Five more babies were born in the little cabin before Hamlet completed the house of brick and stone, a house with a parlor and a piano and a real kitchen—a house with two chimneys and a wide, whitewashed porch. It took awhile. The big red barn came first, then the smokehouse, then the hen coop, then the orchard. But bit by bit the dream ate through the years, surviving every disaster and disappointment, planting its feet into firm reality.

Lydia came and helped me with every baby, and when Phineas gently died in his sleep one day, she buried him in the Pacen cemetery, his treasured war bonnet tucked in beside him, and came to live with us for good. The children

115

call her Aunt Lydie and run to her with all their hurts and pains, confident she will know how to comfort them and cure their ills.

The children. Some are not so much children any more! Through them I can see that the years, though they seem so fleeting, have brought with them constant, uncompromising change.

Pacen has become a substantial little town, spelled Payson now instead of the earlier way. Luxuries, which seemed inconceivable years ago, we accept now as part of life, without thought or question—almost without gratitude. We have the Salem Canal and the Payson Co-op, the telegraph, and even our own brass band. My young ones go each day to the new Square School, and we women are organized into the Relief Society.

We have a brand new City Hall, a tall brick building, and we've even begun construction on our own church. There's a drama society and weekly dances where the band plays quadrilles, French Fours, and Scotch Reels, and the evening ends with a grand midnight supper. I have children old enough for the dancing, and old enough to slip out under the moon and court where the music is only a vague, warm sound.

Since he was an awkward, frustrated, spunky thirteen, my Daniel has been in love with Lucretia Moore. But six months back, Daniel left to serve a mission off in the Southern States with Bill Clayson's boy. Lucretia waits. I notice her at the dances, hanging back, as though to hide her bright, pretty ways. I don't know how deeply Daniel has won her love, how much she is held by the light in his dancing eyes, by the laughter and the music of his voice. That knowledge is locked within her own young heart, waiting to blossom, perhaps as Daniel desires it.

My gentle Deseret has become a woman. Last spring she was sealed to young Moroni Stewart. We drove with them to Salt Lake. It was good to be there. We were able to visit with Hamlet's parents again. Emma was thin and looks frail, but her eyes are good, and she moves with a kind of wiry energy. Daniel's hair is white like a snow-capped mountain, his body just as firm as when he was young, the sparkle in his eye still as warm and delightful. Two of his younger sons live in our valley now, David farming land that touches on our own. It's good to have them, to see a growing family of cousins and nieces and nephews, a family of love and support. Two sons still remain in Salt Lake and they have prospered, so father Drummond has no complaints with the world.

My Jane has spread with the years, become rotund and rosy, and she's just as dear to me as she always was. She lives with her youngest boy, and he tends to spoil her. She knows it and laughs and says that she spoiled him once, and surely it follows that "turn about's fair play." She still comes down and stays with us on occasion. The children love to watch her mother me, and to eat her English tarts and rich plum pudding.

In a lovely room Emma graciously provided, I helped my daughter prepare for her wedding day. Deseret is my eldest girl, and so I called her to me and laid the Wesley mirror in her slender hands, and told her of that other wedding morning when I had stood with no mother by my side and gazed into a future I could not see. We cried together and I drew her close against me, one last time while she was still mine alone.

Then I stood and watched her go where her father waited. He embraced her and I remembered another day when he had lifted the baby girl from the bed beside me.

"She's nearly as pretty as you are," he had said, and his eyes had shone with a love that was beautiful.

I could see that love as he looked on his woman-daughter, and I moved quickly to be by his side when she turned away. For I had seen something else in the gaze he gave her, a pain that only I could know and read. I found his hand and his fingers closed about mine, and we faced the pain together and smiled with her joy.

Twenty years. How could they have passed so quickly, and yet held so much bounty within their hands? Hamlet and I are still young, and sometimes I feel it. My hair is yet thick and brown with no strands of grey. And Hamlet? He still can make my heart start beating when he walks into a room and seeks my eyes, and holds me with the wonder of his gaze. His hair and beard are wheat and corn, sunlight and buttermilk all mingled into one. He is lean and graceful still, and his voice, though older, vibrates like music whenever he chances to speak.

We still know how to ride with the moon and the wind. We have not lost the magic, the ecstasy. He can touch me and I tremble and burn all over. He can kiss me and I feel sweet and eighteen again.

But for all that, we have changed with the land and the children. And the changes have been deep and rich and good.

My handsome, haughty Yanno and his Tasha have become part of our family legend, and so they should be. Lovely Tasha, frozen in story, is young forever, where courage and enchantment will never fade. She bore the baby they both had so desired—a little girl—and Tasha named her Ivy, and Yanno brought her proudly for display. The child was as pretty, as delicate as her mother, and for three happy years she grew in freedom and love, trained by the tender hand of her quiet mother.

Then one day, Tasha slipped while carving up venison and slashed her arm, a deep cut, close to the bone. The cut was not cleaned nor cared for properly; no one understood that the angry red slashes spreading like fingers out and away from the wound meant poisoning of the blood, and death. I didn't even see her to say goodbye. When Yanno came, his eyes wild, his hair unkempt, she was already mourned and buried in proper Ute fashion. Yanno married again. In fact, he took three new brides. Even lumped all together they couldn't begin to match Tasha.

Then one bitter, autumn day nearly two years later, he appeared at my door with a small, tied bundle in one hand and his daughter, Ivy, clinging to the other. She bore my name, he stated with firmness, so now she was to be mine. When I didn't move or reply he dropped his eyes and with more humility than I had ever seen him muster, he asked me to take the girl and give her a home. The squaws were harsh with the child. They refused to teach her. She was too gentle—like her mother. Perhaps my ways would be better for this one.

I knew what he really wanted and couldn't say. I took his anguished face between my hands and reminded him that I had loved her mother and so would love the child, as one of my own. I took the slender hand, so finely made, led the little girl into the house and closed the door. Then I sat with her in my arms and cried and cried.

Ivy has become my real daughter and grown into a sweet and graceful girl. At times, it's hard to remember she's different from the others. Though through the years, Yanno has come consistently, bringing her gifts and carefully teaching her the ways and traditions of her own people, and she has beautifully woven them into her life. As Hamlet so often says, our little Ivy could hold her own in any company.

I know when Daniel comes back from his mission he'll work the land. The land has rubbed into his soul, as it has with his father. The others? My young Adam might well become an animal doctor. He's always the first one there at his father's side to nurse some cow through the night or assist with a calving. He's gentle, yet firm and confident, and very strong willed. Then there's little Jennie who sings like a bird and can coax blossoms out of the desert with just a smile. And Sarah, who can reproduce onto paper any lovely sight she wants to keep, with shading and proportion nearly perfect. Even the evening light when it falls on the mountains, sharp yet mellow, rich yet unsubstantial, can come to life at her fingertips when she wants it to. And Timothy—ah, but it's much too soon to tell yet—too soon to do more than love and listen and watch.

Way back when I carried the twins and Hamlet blessed me, he said I would know that the hand of the Lord was with me. I do. I have felt it so many times through the years. And at times I have even felt my mother's presence, had a sensation that she can see what I'm doing here—that she knows the land, the house, the children—that she's part of each of us, making us all more whole.

There's not one of the children who doesn't love the land, who isn't tied to it in one way or another. So we have planted, and they have begun to reap. Hamlet said it in the beginning, his eyes on fire.

"You and I will be first. We'll start it and build it and watch it grow. And some day when our sons and daughters ask us, we'll tell them that you and I were the first white people to set foot here. No one else plowed or planted or built before us. That's some kind of gift to give your children, Ivy."

So it has come to pass. And the gift is good. But the giving itself is better, and longer-lived. The land goes on; past death the land keeps living. But love keeps living and, unlike the land, love grows. And love alone gives meaning to the land. A family of hearts to keep on beating, generation upon generation, loving and living—and making of the land a home.

Nothing can stop me from welcoming my tomorrows, each new morning with Hamlet there beside me, to keep on giving—to love a little more.